Deliberate Fools

CATHY ANN ROGERS

Aquitaine Ltd
Phoenix, Arizona

Sally J Smith, Editor
Cover design by JD Smith Designs

ISBN-10: 0991484355
ISBN-13: 978-09914843-5-5

www.aquitaineltd.com

Dedication

For all my funny girls, past and present.

O, these deliberate fools! When they do choose
They have the wisdom by their wit to lose.

WILLIAM SHAKESPEARE

The Merchant of Venice

Wednesday Evening

How many years would she get for the killing of a well-meaning friend?
Elizabeth Kearn had murder on her mind when she looked across the table at another perfect match according to one of the popular dating sites. The quality of the constant stream of men over the last two weeks had convinced her that either she had not answered the questions correctly, or the questioning philosophy had a fault. Or was it that she had never found communicating by emails or telephone a substitute for the thrill of immediate physical attraction.

"Elizabeth Kearn, right? I'm Ted Bruce," the man said. He extended both hands, and clasped hers together. "You're much prettier in person."

"Nice to meet you." She extricated her hands from their sweaty captors to take another sip of Chardonnay. Something about wine brought out an edge in her voice that her mother had referred to as her *smart mouth*. The struggle here was to fight to keep a civil tone and not walk away.

This one had crude good looks—dingy blond hair streaked with gray, dusty blue eyes, and thick eyebrows, but his anxious energy had an unattractive quality. He chattered too much, and his nervous sweating reeked of fear. Was she that frightening? She drew a deep breath, and looked into her wine glass before pouring the rich buttery liquid down her throat. *Oh, my kingdom for a man with guts.*

"So, you're new in Phoenix?" he said.

"Several months now," she said.

"How'd you like it so far?"

"It's okay. I like that I won't have to deal with snowstorms."

He paused and reached in toward her. "Do you have any idea how pretty you are? I guess you hear that a lot, but it's the truth."

Elizabeth gave him a weak grin. She wondered if he used the same line at the beginning of every date. Most men did. The words used in lieu of a genuine remark had become so trite as to be meaningless. She bit down on her lip to stifle a caustic remark.

He leaned back in his chair to study her. "I guess someone like you gets tired of hearing that."

"Not necessarily."

"You shy or something? You don't talk much," he said.

Elizabeth remembered another expression her mother used for her. She would say she was *showin' her ass* when she started mouthing back at someone for no good reason. The second glass of wine had dulled her ability to fake a civil tone. *Be nice. Don't say anything rude.*

She looked down into her wine glass again, now empty except for the residual puddle in the bottom. What was the acceptable time limit before she could leave without offending him? She had already finished off two glasses of wine. Much more of this and she would need a third, exceeding her self-imposed limit. She looked beyond Ted's inquiring expression, pausing as she adjusted her tone. Across the room, a couple stood waiting for the hostess. She recognized the man. Walt, her most recent ex-boyfriend, here in the company of another woman.

"I *said* what you do for a living?" he said.

She jumped. "I'm sorry. What did you ask me?"

"What do you do for a living?"

"I manage the Matrix."

"Then why aren't we meeting there? They have great food. I even enjoy the artsy style of the place."

Elizabeth could not admit how embarrassed she would feel to have the staff watch her conduct during a blind date. Not even a blind date, a computer match. "Neutral. I wanted to meet somewhere neutral. Besides, I'm there all the time for work. I like to go somewhere different to relax."

He had a puzzled look on his face. *What could there be not to understand?*

Elizabeth let her eyes wander toward Walt's table while the hostess seated them. She looked back at her date to find him staring at her. "Did you say something?"

Ted Bruce transformed from nervous and anxious to bruised and irritated. "I thought we were having a conversation."

"Sorry," Elizabeth said. But she understood as he probably did that she was not in least bit sorry. She decided she had enough of her online man-shopping spree. Barhopping and one-night stands were beginning to sound appealing.

When he stood, she thought he must have read her mind. He pulled a twenty from his wallet, slapped it down on the table in front of her, and left without a word. No doubt scarred for life. Elizabeth thought she should feel bad, or at least, insulted, not relieved. She waived to her waiter and ordered bruschetta and another glass of wine. No need to pass on good wine and delicious food. Certain to be another flawed decision on her part. Oh, well. The food would soak up the wine, right?

Elizabeth gobbled down most of her artichoke and ham bruschetta, licking her fingers without shame. This would be one of those times she blamed weight gain on her infallible wine-induced hunger spikes. She leaned back, relaxed, and took time to observe the other people in the large dining room. Then she noticed her. She blinked and took a second look. Walt's date, a petite woman with short-cropped hair, glared at her from their table.

Elizabeth looked away. She wanted to look again, but those beady eyes gave her the shivers. She looked down at her plate and picked up her last bite. More likely than not, she had only imagined the woman's stare. She blamed her mood on a combination of the wine and her dissatisfying date. She lifted her eyes from the plate to look again. Walt sat alone now, his date gone or out of view.

Elizabeth turned her attention to her wine glass, debating

on the wisdom of swilling down the remainder when a chill ran through her. She looked up to see this woman walking in her direction. The woman's eyes bore into Elizabeth with their icy stare. She had no doubt the woman meant to intimidate her, either by threat or challenge. Their eyes locked as the woman passed on her way to the restroom. Elizabeth trembled—a ripple of fear overtook her, but she refused to give in to the instinct to run. How dare this stranger bully her. And for what?

When she finished eating and washed down the last drop of wine, Elizabeth tossed her own money next to the twenty and left without looking in Walt's direction. That woman unnerved her. Elizabeth drove home on edge and on alert for a patrol car. Every dark space she passed loomed with danger. Any time now, she expected a petite lunatic to jump out in front of her car and crash through the windshield. Her imagination raged through various scenarios until she pulled inside her garage. When the automatic garage door closed, she relaxed but was still hesitant to leave the protection of the car. She closed her eyes to pull herself together, but all she could see were those eyes. She shivered.

After negotiating with her inner voice about mistaking imaginary threats for reality, she put the incident with the strange little woman behind her and got out of the car. Maybe this had nothing to do with her. She had be a victim of her own wild imagination, again. Her interpretation of events must have been influenced by her current state of mind.

Once she removed her makeup, downed a bottle of water, and made a cup of fennel tea, she settled into her recliner and pressed the call button with her best friend's photo.

"Well, Esmeralda Dearing. I still haven't met a man worth waxing my legs for."

"Elizabeth, you need to have a better attitude," Esme said. "These poor bastards don't know what they're in for when they meet up with you."

"I'm finished begging for love. If it's not easy, I don't want to bother. And I'm not interested in coaxing them out of their shells."

"You don't have to beg. Just pant a little." Esme started laughing. Elizabeth could not stay mad long and started to chuckle. "Whatever happened to Walt? You two got on alright for a while."

"It's funny you ask. I saw him at the restaurant tonight with an odd little woman who gave me the heebie-jeebies."

"Why? Did you go over to say hello?"

"I might have if she hadn't given me the evil eye."

"You're a pretty girl, but you've got to get over this paranoia that everyone is staring at you. It was probably nothing. I bet you were still in a mood over your date and transferred your emotions onto her."

"Thank you, Dr. Phil. I'll remember that the next time another deranged lunatic looks at me as if she wants to murder me. Speaking of murder, don't think you're safe for talking me into this online dating adventure."

"You just need a better attitude. One day, you'll meet Mr. Right."

"That's the trouble. I already have. Six times," Elizabeth paused. "Shush. I think I heard a noise."

"What kind of noise?"

"Stop talking for a minute!" Elizabeth walked back toward her kitchen, straining to hear the sound in her head to figure out from which room it came. Then she heard it again. A metallic clunk echoed from the garage end of the house. She tiptoed through the dark kitchen, listening, alert, and unsure if she should be scared.

When she reached the garage, she picked up a hammer left on the counter and turned on the lights. Nothing looked disturbed, but she had to be sure. She walked the perimeter of the garage, looking for anything suspicious, anything different, but saw nothing disturbed.

She relaxed, convinced that the sound came from the outside. Esme must be right. That awful date put her in a mood that tainted everything else. She turned to go back inside the house when she saw something move in her peripheral vision. She turned to look. A red fluid seeped between the upper stack panels of the garage door. The heavy smell came into her nostrils as she drew closer.

"That smells like paint," Elizabeth said.

"What?" Esme said, her digitized voice emanating from Elizabeth's hip where she held the phone.

She raised the phone to her ear. "There's paint oozing into my garage from the outside. Hold on. I'm going to see what's going on." Esme yelled for her to stop, but Elizabeth set the phone down on a shelf, and went out the man door to get to the front of the garage.

"Don't go out there." Esme's voice was barely audible, and Elizabeth ignored her.

Edgar Hamilton smiled. He liked to think of his money as tiny soldiers he sent out to work every day to build his empire. Money gave him opportunity, not only security. Freedom would come later, at least that is what he hoped. But now, what he appreciated the most was having the means to hire someone to do a job he could not accomplish on his own—finding people.

He heard of Sam Shelton from a friend who had needed proof of his cheating wife. According to Monty, Sam had an eccentric reputation, old-fashioned, but the best private investigator around. Now with Internet access literally at his fingertips, Sam left his competition in the dust. No one could hide from him once he started searching. With accolades like that, Edgar was surprised to hear that he did not mess around running up a bill for his more affluent clients. Just because you can afford to pay more does not mean you should. That had always been a philosophy Edgar embraced.

Once he made up his mind, Edgar had to wait a week for an evening appointment. He checked his watch. Eight, and right on time. Edgar watched Sam's six foot two build emerge from an inner office. His balding head, flushed round face, and piercing gray eyes gave him a misleading comical appearance. Monty had warned Edgar that Sam had dispensed with any semblance of a professional appearance, and wore sweats, even when he met clients. Today was no different.

The office looked exactly as Edgar had imagined. He thought that his wife, Donna, would call this style *shabby shriek*. The worn leather love seat in the reception area looked as if it had never met a cleaning cloth. Dust layered the side table next to a lone wooden chair across the room. The reception desk, that Edgar thought was there to give the illusion of a secretary, contained a cluttered stack of file folders and loose paperwork, except for a small area cleared in the center as if the missing, or misplaced, receptionist needed the space to create more paperwork. Edgar sniffed at the mustiness, although he tried not to. He was not here to hire a housekeeper.

Sam sauntered toward him, extending a sweaty palm meant as a welcoming gesture. True to his reputation, the detective wore blue sweats with white socks and leather sandals.

"Come on in, Edgar. Nice weather, isn't it. Monty tells me you have a job for me, but didn't say what. Here, have a seat." Sam lifted the contents of one of the chairs in front of his desk and set it all down on the floor in a loud thump next to other similar piles. "It's a good thing folks don't hire me to be organized. Course, I know where everything is." He laughed and winked.

Edgar smiled. This man knew his own faults, acknowledged them, and put you at ease about it at once. The inner office was more cluttered and stuffy than the outer office. Although he could not see the dust, Edgar suspected it lurked between the pages of the dozens of files around the perimeter on the' office floor.

"Well," Edgar began hesitantly. "I want you to find a woman for me. Let me rephrase that. I want you to locate the whereabouts of a woman I used to know about six years ago."

"Name?" Sam poised a pen over a notepad and started to write.

"Elizabeth Kearn."

"Age?"

"Thirty six or thirty-seven."

"Last known address?"

"Here in downtown Denver. I don't recall the address, but she lived on Girard."

"Occupation?"

"She was a waitress, but I remember she was trying to get an assistant manager job at a different restaurant."

"Any known family or friends"

"None that we talked about. We kept to ourselves mostly when we were seeing each other."

"It shouldn't be too difficult to find her. Even if she's married, I should still be able to track her through marriage licenses."

Edgar felt a pang of panic. Why had he not thought this through? Of course, she could very well be married. Edgar flinched at his lack of foresight and his transparency in front of Sam.

"Any particular reason you're looking for this woman?"

"Nostalgia, I guess. This is probably a mistake since you never know what you'll find looking up someone you haven't seen in a while, but what the heck."

"Sure. I'll call you tomorrow and let you know what I've found out."

"Tomorrow? That's quick, isn't it?"

"Not if you know what you're doing." Sam stood and reached out his hand to Edgar in a tactful dismissal.

"Thanks, Sam. This means a lot to me."

Edgar left the way he came in, but Sam did not escort him to the door. Now that he had made this real by taking action, he wondered if he were insane. What crazy impulse made him think finding her could change his life? What if the reunion went well, or did not? Would Elizabeth even want to see him? If she did not, he would have no one else to blame but himself.

Edgar pushed the elevator call button. He straightened his back, took in a deep breath, and let out a nervous chuckle. He strode into the elevator when the doors slid open. He had time to work this out. Sam could not possibly find someone overnight that he had searched for without success for six months.

Elizabeth woke up on the driveway outside her garage on cue with the arrival of a police cruiser. The flaring lights half blinded her. She started to lift her head and shoulders. An officer rushed over to her to help her stand. Normally, she considered accepting assistance a sign of feminine weakness, but she had trouble steadying herself, her throbbing temples keeping her off balance. The strong arms that raised her like a ragdoll distracted her from the confusion until he spoke.

"Can you stand on your own? We should get you to the hospital to check out that gash on your head."

"Please, no. I think I'm okay. I just need to sit down."

He gave her a skeptical look that told her he had seen bravado before. "We'll talk about that later. Can you tell me what happened?"

Elizabeth squinted. "I was talking to my friend on the phone when I thought I heard a noise in the garage. I came out here, and, oh yeah, I smelled something funny then noticed paint dripping through the garage door. I opened the man door to see what was happening. That's the last thing I remember. I don't know how I got out here."

"Take a look," he said. He turned her toward the garage door then aimed the beam from his flashlight over a series of letters hand-painted across the width of her garage door. She went weak in the knees when the meaning sunk in. WHORE. She leaned against him for support and kept a tight grip on his arm. Jeez, this man was solid as a building. "From the smell, this isn't the water-based type of paint you can hose off. Have you had any threats or fallout with someone recently?"

"No. This is crazy. I can't think of anyone who dislikes me. That much, anyway."

"Think about it on your way to the hospital. You might not want to go, but you've been hit hard, and you were unconscious."

"I guess you're right. I do feel sick to my stomach, and my head is pounding worse than when I first came to."

"We'll need a full statement, but that can wait until you get medical attention."

She spotted the flares of the ambulance lights as the vehicle turned onto her street. When she stepped into the back of the ambulance, she looked at her garage door. The letters had a neon effect in the intermittent lights of the emergency LED bar.

I can only wonder what my neighbors will say.

Thursday Morning

Good to his word, Sam rang Edgar first thing the next morning. Edgar blinked to wake up, and then grabbed his phone.

"Sam Shelton here. I hope it's not too early."

Edgar's heartbeat quickened. "Not at all."

"I have the information you wanted on the girl."

"So soon?"

"I said I would, didn't I?" Edgar thought he caught a tone of indignation in his reply.

"I didn't mean I doubted you, but I've been searching for months and thought finding her might be difficult."

"You didn't know how to look. First, she's not married. No children. She was a bookkeeper for the Dome Restaurant. She moved from Denver's LoDo District, that apartment on Girard Place she lived when she knew you, to Phoenix, Arizona six months ago. The company decided to open a restaurant in downtown Phoenix and sent her to supervise the opening. The Matrix Restaurant opened a month ago, but from what I can tell, she's staying on there as the manager. I've texted you the restaurant address and number, and her personal number and address. She's living in a gated community close to the restaurant."

"I'm impressed."

"Just doing my job. I'll send you a final statement to your business email."

Edgar heard the text and email notifications. His insides prickled. No excuses now. He found a quick flight to Phoenix, booked a choice room at one of the larger downtown hotels, and pulled out his to-go bag. When he sat in his first class seat on the plane and, at last, stopped the constant motion, he experienced a moment of panic, doubt in his decision. He took a deep breath when the attendant approached him, smiled, and ordered a drink. This all happened so fast, he blinked to make sure he was awake. He knocked back his insecurity. He would apply determination to this situation as he did to attain any goal. *Make this happen.*

Edgar unpacked his suitcase to settle his nerves. Looking down at the bag's interior, he thought how Donna's habits mirrored her personality—every item tightly lined up by type and color, crisp and organized, practical, no room for whimsy or disarray. Then he rewound her reaction to this trip.

"Go on and get this out of your system. I'm not worried. I'm the one who lives in your present. She's only a misty memory of another lifetime. I've heard that men get dreamy and sentimental about past relationships when they hit middle age, and that's fine. Just remember that I'm your wife, and I'm not going anywhere without a fight. So go on and have your fling. I'll be waiting here when you get back."

"You make that sound like a threat."

"Maybe it is," she said.

Her confidence annoyed him. Changing your life was complicated, but he expected that. The point Donna did not comprehend was her end would be the same no matter how the reunion went with Elizabeth. Happy people do not look outside their marriage for other relationships. He knew that as much as he knew anything. As competent as she was, she had to know neither of them were in love and probably never had been.

He made his way down the small streets to Presidents Boulevard in the center of the Phoenix downtown district, and paused at the stunning black glass door with a crystal door handle. He blew out a quiet whistle when he saw the spectacular interior. A semi-spiral staircase led to the second floor loft with tables edged against the railings. Downstairs, bistro tables filled the center floor surrounded by intimate booths around the perimeter. Edgar noted that the seating offered every patron a view of the large plasma screens. A modern acrylic bar extended from the entrance to a kitchen.

A hostess with a vacant smile asked if he wanted a table, a booth, or a seat at the bar.

"One of the booths, please. And I'd like to speak with Elizabeth, if she's free. I'm an old friend from Denver. I took a chance she'd be working."

"Yes, she's in the office. I'll get her after I seat you. Would you like a drink while you're waiting?"

"Yes, I would."

"What would you like? I'll have your server bring it right over."

"Chivas on the rocks."

She smiled at him in what struck Edgar as a human response more than the mechanical gestures acquired by individuals in public service.

Now that Elizabeth would be here any minute, he had no idea about what to say to her. He flushed when he saw her coming toward him. Her beauty was not as delicate as he remembered, but she still had the same blonde hair, slim body, and catlike demeanor. She still had great legs, and still not afraid to show them off in her black miniskirt. *Wow.*

He saw confusion and then what was that look—disappointment? He should not feel hurt, but she looked at him as she would a stranger to her. His rehearsed lines failed him so that when she stopped in front of him, he could barely talk. His words sounded dry and awkward.

"Elizabeth, I guess you don't remember me," Edgar said. He knew he was starting to sweat and hoped she did not notice his shaking hands.

"Edgar? Is that you? I can't believe it. You're the last person I expected."

Good, she remembers me. "Yes, it's me. How've you been?"

"I've been good if you smooth over the rough spots. What brings you to Phoenix? I assume you're still working for *that* company. Are you here on a business trip?"

Was it his imagination, or did she look nervous, too. She slid into the seat opposite him and smiled. Her bright pink lips, still full and inviting, held partly open, triggered the intimate memories from their past.

"Not business." He hesitated. "I wanted to see you again."

As soon as the words were out of his mouth, he regretted the disclosure. Her face had an alarmed expression, but she quickly smoothed that back into a warm smile.

"That's very sweet. I never expected to see you again. What's been going on to bring on this nostalgia?"

"Well, I got the job, and then got married. No children, big house, expensive cars, nothing out of the ordinary. It's stable, predictable, and boring."

"That's what you wanted, isn't it? *Your dream.*" Yes, he heard bitterness in her reply, but she had the right.

"Getting what you want isn't all you expect, especially when your life lacks vigor and spontaneity. So, what happened to your head?"

Elizabeth touched the bandage on the side of her head. "It's a long story. Nothing too serious."

"That sounds mysterious."

"I think it makes me look interesting, don't you?"

"You look interesting to me with or without the bandage."

She blushed then lowered her eyes. "Are you having a meal?"

"I need to eat, but it would be nice to have company. Can you?"

"Sure. Why not."

"Good. Then you can tell me the story behind the head dressing."

Elizabeth whipped out her cell phone the minute he left the restaurant and called Esme.

"You're not going to believe it. Edgar Hamilton came in to see me this evening."

"You're kidding. I remember you told me he dumped you because you weren't corporate wife material."

"That's the one."

"So, how's the blast from the past?"

Elizabeth hesitated. "I'm not sure. I haven't processed it yet. He *says* he wants me back as soon as he divorces his wife."

"Wife! I thought you said he was smart."

"He claims he only married her to fit the part, but he knows now he never loved her. Jeez, it sounds less believable when I repeat it."

"They all claim that they never really loved their wives. Only married because she was knocked up, was rich, prominent, or influential. They may be telling the truth, but that leaves you wondering if any hookup with a man like that would be sincere."

"Not too far off from what I've been thinking."

"So how'd you leave it?"

"I'm a fool, but I told him I'd consider getting back together, but that I wouldn't promise anything. After all, he ripped my heart out before, and I don't think I've healed yet."

Elizabeth knew what Esme's silence meant—it's your life!

"It's the bang on your head last night," Esme said. "You've got selective amnesia. Remembering all the good and stuffing the bad."

"We all do that. I bet you have a man out there you can't get out of your system."

"Elizabeth, when you want to get something out of your system, you take a laxative."

They both started laughing until Elizabeth had tears running down her cheeks. Esme had to be the funniest woman alive. If she made money by the wisecrack, she would be a millionaire.

"I've got to get back to work," Elizabeth said. "It's almost closing time. Will you be up later?"

"Sure, until one or so," Esme said. "I wish we didn't live in two states, or I'd be waiting for you when you got home."

"I know. I feel the same way."

"Talk to you in a few. In the meantime, don't take anymore wooden nickels." Esme disconnected. For Elizabeth, the distance between them never seemed farther.

Thursday Evening

Walt Perry sat across from Patti Slocum at a different restaurant tonight. He made sure he picked one where he could avoid Elizabeth. Last night, Patti showed her true jealous nature. He hoped Elizabeth had not noticed them or had seen the way Patti watched her. She had gone a little psycho. That was just too much. He could not drop her off fast enough after that.

"So, you've eaten here before?" Patti said.

"A few times. The food's good."

"Did you come here with *her*?"

"No, as a matter of fact, but so what if I did?"

Patti said nothing, but looked amused while she read the menu. Funny, Walt thought, how he had instantly felt masterful over her small size and shyness when they first met. That soon changed as he got to know her better. She was a strong-willed, opinionated snob. She corrected him too often and frequently told him he needed to go to college. She had even started making all of the decisions about their dates, unlike this evening. She had even lost her comeliness. That was saying something considering his appetite. Loss of sex appeal was the deal breaker in his relationships.

"I bought tickets for a lecture after dinner. It's about art and politics in the nineteenth century."

He couldn't help himself. "Sounds like a riot."

Patti shook her head. "Sarcasm noted. Don't take that attitude. This is good for you to broaden your intellectual horizons. You'll see."

His eyes glazed over throughout the half-hour lecture. He continued to tune her out during the drive afterward, while she rambled on about the merits of using art to express political opinion. He drove quietly and intently until they arrived in front of her house.

"Coming in?"

"No."

"Suit yourself. Call me tomorrow. I want to tell you about a couple of weekend seminars in Sedona we can attend. You'll enjoy them."

"Right. Tomorrow." With the car engine running, he reached across to open her door and then watched her until he saw she reached the front porch.

As he drove slowly away from her house, he caught her in his rear-view mirror watching after him. He liked that image of seeing her image receding behind him.

Patti sensed Walt's change of attitude, but she set it aside unconcerned. He was showing resistance to the education she provided him, but that would pass. It was obvious he was really into her and wanted to please her. She made hot chocolate, and stared out onto her back yard. *And no woman from his past would have the opportunity to interfere with that.*

Breathing in the fresh citrus blossoms hovering near the front door, Patti checked the mailbox she had ignored the last three days. Nothing but bills and more bills. She tossed the small stack into the inbox on her desk and started to turn her attention elsewhere when she noticed two lavender invitation envelopes mingled with the others. The sender had printed her name in neat block letters, squared yet feminine in thin strokes. No return address, but the envelopes, with their inviting fragrance, powdery and floral, had a friendly, benign quality that intrigued her. She regarded them and tried to recognize the handwriting or guess the organization hosting the event.

The two invitations stood out for another reason—no postmark on the stamps. She wondered who had walked them here—and when. The mailbox had no lock, so anyone passing could pop a note or letter inside at practically any time. She studied the envelopes a few minutes before she reached for the letter opener and sliced open both.

Her anticipation turned to alarm when she saw the contents of the first one. A chill of terror pierced her body. After several minutes, she calmed herself and reread the frightening words, her hands shaking the paper as she read:

> *As said before, you tart and whore,*
> *the time has come for penance.*
> *Your silence tells your victim's hell*
> *now passing down your sentence.*
> *You cannot flee or hope to be*
> *free from our decision.*
> *By Friday next this written text*
> *will tell the death incision.*

Who in Phoenix could hate her this much to want to kill her? She considered not looking in the other envelope, but decided it best to know the worst. She reached inside and tore out the note.

> *You have been charged with willful and intentional destruction of an innocent child. This court gives you until Sunday to respond to the charges by making a full disclosure of your actions in public by*

17

newspaper and television. The jury of your peers has granted you a life sentence if you comply. If not, your sentence is death. You cannot hope to escape our judgment.

Panic. Sunday? Which Sunday? She had not checked or opened mail in a while. She knew of a child who died, but she had not murdered her. Call the police. She picked up the cordless telephone on her desk and dialed 911. When she put the receiver to her ear, she heard nothing. She went to the other telephones in the house and found none to be working. She had not taken her cell phone with her on her date, and now she could not find it. She had no way to call for help.

Her next instinct was to leave the house. She picked up her purse and keys and went to the garage. The car would not start, but groaned and strained as if it were out of gas. She needed to get a neighbor to help her. She used the garage door opener, but it did not respond. The manual override did not work either when she pulled on the long cord attached to the mechanism on the ceiling.

Stay calm. She went back inside the house to leave by a different door, but no exit would open. Neither did the first-floor windows. She could not even break the window glass since she had replaced all first-floor windows with shatterproof glass last year for extra security. Upstairs, she found the situation just as hopeless since the only way down was to jump from the second-story windows. No windows led out to the garage roof, and she had all the trees cut back far enough away from the windows to prevent burglar's access. She had worried so much about intruders, she had not considered escaping.

The letter writer must be in this house somewhere. She ran for the revolver she kept in her nightstand, but the drawer was empty. She ran downstairs to the kitchen for something to use for protection, but found all her best kitchen knives missing. *How did someone get in here and remove my stuff?* She stood in the hallway trying to think of what to do next. Then she smiled. Of course, her secret bunker.

Thanks to taking the partial liquidation on the annuity from her structured settlement, she not only purchased a beautiful home in the Encanto-Palmcroft Historic District, but had enough left over to install a panic room in an area in the basement set off from the rest of the floor plan. Its end wall had a concealed door disguised with industrial shelving. She had stocked up on emergency food and supplies, including a portable toilet. The space was secret and secure. That would be the place to hide.

She rushed through the kitchen and down the stairs to the basement. After pressing the panic button to make sure the house went into emergency mode and sent a message to the police, she slipped into her safe room. She had little peace of mind, however. How would she know when it would be safe to come out?

The trouble with secret rooms, she realized, is that there was a good chance no one would look for her in a room that was not supposed to exist. Once barricaded safely inside without means to communicate with the outside world, she had made herself a prisoner. Not getting that landline in the safe room was another false economy.

Walt had arrived home, still annoyed and antagonistic toward Patti and their relationship. He slipped on a pair of pajama bottoms, grabbed a can of beer, and sat to watch the game he recorded earlier. Then he heard a knock on his door. He peeked through the peephole and saw a shiny badge with an officer attached behind it.

Walt opened the door. "Yes?"

"Walt Perry?"

"That's me."

"Can we come in? We'd like to ask you a few questions about Patti Slocum."

Walt tried to hold back his anger. "So what kind of game is she playing now?"

The two officers exchanged looks. The first one said, "She hit her panic button, but when we arrived at her home, she was not there. When we interviewed some of the neighbors, we learned you dropped her off about an hour ago."

"That's right. We went to dinner and a lecture, and then I took her home."

"A lecture?"

Walt flushed. How emasculating. "Yes, some lecture on art and politics. Her idea."

"So have you talked with her since you dropped her at home?"

"No. There's no reason to."

"What would you say about her mood? Anything bothering her? Did she mention being afraid of someone?"

"No. Just the opposite." Walt started to feel uneasy. Why were they asking him about her? "She probably hit the button by accident."

"If that were the case, where is she? Her security company has not received a call from her to alert them of a false alarm. Would you have any objections if we looked around?"

"I guess not. What do you think? That you'll find her hiding in one of my closets?"

"Just being thorough."

"Go ahead."

The second officer, who had stood in the background, took off around the small house peeking in closets, looking behind every door, then out to his garage.

"Have you been dating Miss Slocum long?"

"A few months."

"Get along okay. Any significant arguments?"

"Not any that come to mind."

"Did she ever mention anyone she had a disagreement with, or someone who might have threatened her?"

"No. She never talks about anything other than art. I don't say much of anything."

"What about relatives?"

"She has a mother who lives in London. I've never met her. Patti doesn't talk about her much, so I assume they aren't close."

"I see," the officer said, but Walt did not see.

"You must have an idea about what happened to her. Someone must have seen something. Her neighbors seem to see everything else."

"All they saw was your car dropping her off and driving away slowly. They claim she had no other visitors, at least from the front."

"So you're thinking I killed her or something?"

"We're fact gathering. We don't know if she's dead or if someone's harmed her in any way. We need to determine what happened before we jump to conclusions."

Friday Early Afternoon

After a drawn-out interview with police detectives, Walt worried they still did not believe him. He had explained how he felt that evening and how he had not gone inside but left her at the door. He told them his intention had been to end it with her, but he had wanted to postpone the big break-up scene to another time. Talking about wanting to get rid of her the same night she went missing did not look good for him. Men had been convicted on less.

Phoenix was not like Corinth, Kentucky. He knew few people here, and had no real friends yet. The only person he knew well was Elizabeth. He could not be sure what kind of reception he would get from her, but he had to chance it. She might be able to help him. At the least, direct him to a good lawyer.

He cleaned up and set off around one-thirty. He knew her routine from picking her up there many times, and knew the place would not be busy after two. He chose a booth to the side and scanned the room until he spotted her. His spirits sank. He did not see her at first, but when he did, he saw her embracing a tall, handsome man. Their familiarity was obvious from the way they held on to each other as they talked. She walked the man to the front, he kissed her cheek, and left.

It was not as if he did not expect her to date again, so he was surprised seeing her with another man rattled him. He had decided to slip out the side exit when she saw him. Too late now.

"Walt, is that you?" Elizabeth's familiar voice floated across the room like music. Then, he jumped when a hand touched his shoulder. The waitress attached to it stepped into his view.

"Hey, darlin', we haven't seen you in a while."

"Hi, Dolo," he said. "How are you?"

"You remembered my nickname. I'm flattered. I've been fine. Making money. You know this place. Always busy. So how are you?"

"I've been busy, too."

"I assume you're here to see Elizabeth. I'll get her for you. Oh, she already saw you. Here she comes."

He groaned and forced a smile. When Elizabeth walked up, she looked confused, but not annoyed, as he might have expected.

"Hi, Elizabeth. Have you being doing alright?"

"Great. I haven't seen you around here in a while, but I guess you can't stay away from the good food for long, huh."

"That, too, but I actually wanted to talk to you. Before you get worried I'm stalking you or something," he said quickly when he saw her face tense up, "I have a problem, and I don't know who to go to for help."

Suddenly, her face was soft again, a kindly concern—her expression gentle and caring. Those same lovely eyes he remembered. He stifled back memories of her face close to his, her penetrating look. *Stay on point.*

"It's so bizarre that I almost cannot believe it. A woman I've been seeing is missing. The police questioned me as if they believe I had something to do with it. I think I need a good lawyer."

"Is that the woman I saw you with the other night?"

Walt flushed. "Yes, and I'm sorry about that. I made the mistake of pointing you out, and I guess she got jealous."

"Forget it. These things are bound to happen. But tell me why the police suspect you?"

He recounted the events of the evening, including the last time he saw her in his rearview mirror, omitting his uncharitable thoughts. "Then, I let them search my house. They didn't find anything, but still. I sure didn't kill her, but I'm worried that if she turns up dead, they'll come right after me."

"What do you know about her?"

"Not a lot. I never asked her much about her family or past relationships. Most of our time, she spent reminding me I wasn't as smart as she was and talking about art."

Elizabeth went thoughtful for several seconds, seeming to calculate something in her mind. Finally, after what seemed like hours, she said, "It sounds like finding out more about her might be the solution. I mean, if the police are just looking at you as an obvious subject in some domestic dispute and don't know much about her past, I can see how bad it looks for you. Let's see what we can find out about her from what you know. Once we have those facts lined up, we can do a search for her online."

"I'm afraid I don't know how to do that."

"Don't worry. I do. Write down all you know. We'll get on my computer and start looking. Everyone has history. Maybe she has more of a past than the average person does. For example, she could have been involved in a drunk driving accident and hurt someone. Or she could have a violent ex-husband. Or she could have robbed a bank and neglected to share the loot with her gang."

"Now, you're just being silly," he said.

"Seriously, you never know here in Phoenix. Many folks come here to escape their lives and to reinvent themselves. The trouble is we can't escape who we really are. We repeat our same habits and patterns. What if your friend was like that? I mean, *is* like that."

"That's an interesting angle. I'd been thinking she could've been a victim of random violence. Wrong place at the wrong time."

"That could still be the case, but we have to find something to take the focus off you and onto more appropriate scenarios."

"Okay. When do you have free time so we can get together?"

"I take my afternoon break at two and won't need to come back until six. Can you meet me at my place about two fifteen?"

"Sure. I really appreciate this, Elizabeth."

"Write down the basics. You know the type of stuff, name and address. Don't worry. We'll figure this out," she said, and placed her hand on his shoulder.

"See you at two fifteen then."

While she waited for Walt, Elizabeth listened to soothing music with a glass of *demi- panaché*. She had already slipped into her favorite worn-out sweats and sat in front of her laptop at the kitchen table when Walt arrived, carrying a notebook and her favorite wine.

"A thank-you gift for helping me. Having someone to talk to has relieved my mind. I appreciate this."

"No problem. Have a seat, and let me see what you got."

Walt handed her his notes. He had jotted down where they met, places they went, her full name, address, car make and model, but not much else.

"Who are you, Patty Slocum?" Elizabeth whispered. Having had the unpleasant experience of being under Patti's scrutiny, Elizabeth knew that she would recognize her if she popped up. She typed the name in the search box, hit the little magnifying glass, and waited. She found split references to genealogical websites, but no other results. *So you're a real nobody.* That was mean-spirited of her, but she savored the possibility that this woman had something to hide. She certainly had no business being jealous, but she admitted that when she read he had met Patti at the art museum, that stung. He must have a habit of picking up women meditating in front of paintings. She had thought that theirs was a chance meeting, kismet. Instead, she had been the target of a cheap pickup routine. Not too flattering.

"Nothing's coming up," she said.

"I don't understand that. She talked about being involved in so many cultural auxiliary committees that I would think she'd be mentioned often enough to come up in searches."

"I'll check her telephone number," she said. The phone number showed private. "We can't confirm her phone without purchasing from the search site. Even if we paid, we don't have a guarantee we'd learn more about her."

Elizabeth did not think anyone could hide in the twenty-first century with instant communication and data availability, but she had been wrong before.

"Maybe I've not hit on the right search. I'll check the Maricopa County Assessor's website. We can find her through her property. We might not have the right spelling of her name. Sometimes, people use a nickname as their real name with friends, but you can't do that on legal documents." She searched for properties under that name, the last name, and then by the address Walt had given her.

"Look at this. Her home is listed under a different name, Abigail Bradley." She made a note of the name. "Do you think she's actually renting the house?"

"The house isn't hers? That's strange," Walt said. "She told me she put a lot of money into renovating, like adding that second floor."

Elizabeth saw Walt lose all color in his face. He is taking this hard, she thought. Finding out someone has tricked you is not something everyone can handle, but she would be more angry than shocked if she found out a man lied about owning his home.

"Maybe this Abigail is fronting for her. Like Patti let Abigail put the property in her name for some reason. Sure is mysterious," Elizabeth said. She took another sip. "I've got it. Why don't we find her mother? She would know where her daughter is."

"Patti said her mother's name is Verna Kilgore. She's been married a couple of times, but she's a widow now."

Elizabeth perked up. "Good, something to search for." She started pounding the keys to do a general search, looking for the name in social sites. She was surprised to see so many older members on these sights, posting recipes, showing off grandchildren and pets, probably the first time in history multiple generations popularized the same interest. "On the rolling search screen, Elizabeth stopped when she saw a photo of an older version of the woman she saw at the restaurant.

"Walt, look at this."

"Dang. That looks like Patti, all right. But that's not possible. This woman's too old."

"Keep up, Walt. Not too old to be her mother." Elizabeth clicked on the photo and went straight to a popular social site. "Look, her name is Verna Kilgore. She has to be Patti's mother."

Walt looked at the profile. "But this woman lives in Kentucky."

Elizabeth grinned. This was delicious. "Yeah, *London*, Kentucky."

"Oh, my… You're right. So Patti's turned out to be a real phony in more ways than one."

"Sure has." She saw the woman had a public profile and started scrolling down to find out more about her. Fortunately, she was active on the site and provided almost a daily record of her life. "Look, she moved to Phoenix. She's right here in town. I bet that's where Missy Patti is—at Mommy's place."

Elizabeth started typing again. This time, she found a telephone listing for Verna Kilgore with an address. "Walt, write down this address. We're going to pay her a visit."

They were disappointed to find no one at home at the address. They peeked around the backyard, but they could not even find a pet. Elizabeth thought Walt looked relieved, but dismissed it. None of this has been easy on him. Probably how he copes.

"It's just as well," Walt said. "I'll give this new information to the cops. They can track her down. Well, I think this solves the mystery. They must be somewhere together. Hitting the panic button had to be an accident after all."

"Right. A bit anticlimactic, but at least this'll take the heat off you. Here," Elizabeth reached inside her purse and pulled out a business card. "Just as a precaution, here's an attorney that comes into the restaurant. He's good. Call him if anything new happens."

Elizabeth stopped at her house so Walt could get his truck. She saw him pause and she stiffened.

"Thanks for being there for me," he said. "I owe you."

"You're welcome, Walt" Elizabeth said, relieved. "See you around the restaurant some time."

She saw him wave when he backed up. She worried about him. The news of Patti telling so many lies affected him more than she would have expected from such a resilient man.

What a weird afternoon. Maybe I shouldn't wish for excitement.

Friday Early Evening

Elizabeth sat across from Edgar and admired the view from the Patina Restaurant set on the top of Sorrell Mountain in North Phoenix. When she looked back at him, she met his eyes.

"What're you thinking about?" he said.

"I'm thinking about how you impressed me when we met. Intelligent, ambitious, focused, and handsome. Just enough confidence to make you charming rather than arrogant."

"I sound irresistible."

"You were," she said.

"Past tense?"

"I still admire you. I'm happy you've accomplished your goals, but I'm not sure I want to start up again with a man who left me because I wasn't good enough." She watched him go pale and had a moment of sadistic pleasure in his discomfort.

"Sometimes we make bad choices that seemed right at the time. I thought a conventional wife would get me further in the company. I know I made a mistake. That doesn't mean I have to keep paying for that selfish decision the rest of my life." He raised his wine glass in a mock toast and took a sip.

"Why are you really back? What do you want from me?"

"I told you. I want to find out my chances of winning you back. I want to make up for what I did." He reached over to touch her lightly on her hand. "I was such a fool to let you go."

"You want absolution? Okay. I absolve you. But only for the past."

The waiter approached and Edgar moved his hand. They looked at their menus, gave the waiter their orders, and watched him disappear into the kitchen.

"Well?" Elizabeth said.

"Well," he said. "Where does this trip down memory lane take us? Is that what you're thinking? Are you asking yourself if it's possible to go back in time like the last several years hadn't happened?"

"Those years did happen. Tell me, does your wife know that you're here and why?"

Edgar looked uncomfortable. A little less in control than he had been a minute before, she noticed. "She knows I'm reevaluating my life," he said.

"You realize I can't take you seriously while you're still married. You're not in a position to start up a relationship with me or anyone else. Unless that's the type of man you've become."

Edgar's face lost color. "You're right. I'm still selfish and more impatient. But we can be friends again, can't we?"

"Friends? We were never anything like friends before. We were two people having a sexual relationship. Now, we're ex-lovers, not a couple of former gal pals who used to share shopping adventures, and ran into each other at afternoon tea." She let out a loud sigh. Time to change the subject before she gave him one of her caustic comments. Pretend the past did not happen? Right, like that could happen. She shifted in her seat, and gave him a defiant look.

"Speaking of friends who are really ex-lovers, a man I used to date needed my help today. The police think he did away with his girlfriend, so I told him I'd help him."

Edgar aimed an irritated glare at her at the abrupt shift in their conversation. "How are you planning to help him?"

"Looking into this woman's past. I saw her once only the other night. She creeped me out. I thought there might be something about her past to tell us why she might need to disappear. We worked on it this afternoon, but we didn't get too far. She doesn't have a big history on the Internet, but at least we found her mother."

"This afternoon?"

"Yeah. Walt came to the restaurant, so I invited him over to my place during my break so we could try to find out something about her."

She watched Edgar He had not changed. She knew he was picturing her alone with another man and thinking the worst.

"I could help with that," Edgar said.

"How?"

"I know a private investigator who can do a thorough search on her in a short time, if he's available."

"That'd be great, but neither of us can afford that kind of expense."

"I think I could manage his fee as a favor to you."

"So I would be obligated to you?" Elizabeth said. She gave him a wry grin. "That's a generous gesture, but I'd better make sure Walt's okay with that."

"He asked for help, didn't he? He doesn't seem too proud."

"I know how he must sound to someone who doesn't know him," Elizabeth said. "Walt's not a bad guy. He's all right."

"If he's such a great guy, why aren't you still seeing him?"

"He got a little too possessive and clingy when we went out. That behavior makes me nervous, so I ended it. Other than that, we had a lot of fun together, and got along great. I don't have a problem helping him."

"Give me the information you know so far. Sam will dig up the rest."

"I guess Walt won't mind. He doesn't have anybody out here. I'm sure he'll be grateful for whatever help he can get. Now, let's see. Her name is Patti Slocum. She doesn't seem to work. Here's her address." She pulled a notepad from her purse and tore off the top sheet with an address scribbled across it. "Your detective might want to know that I tried a cross search with her name and address, but nothing came up. Then, we went through county records, birth records, and general Internet search. Nothing. Walt was positive she owned her house, but when I typed in her address, the county assessor's website shows Abigail Bradley owns it. He thought that was very strange. Oh, give your shamus that name, too. She might be a friend."

"Was he at your place long?"

"An hour or two," she said, ignoring that subtle interrogation technique she remembered from their past. "It's amazing how trusting we are. We tend to believe whatever strangers tell us about themselves. Do you know that she told him her mother lived in London?"

"What about it?"

"Get this. Her mother lives, or lived, in London, *Kentucky*, not London, *England*. Walt said Patti is a bit of a snob, puts on airs. I guess she wanted to give the impression she comes from money."

"What do you mean, lives or lived?"

"Her mother, Verna Kilgore, has a place here in Phoenix, but she still has a current address in Kentucky. We're thinking there's a good chance Patti's here in town hiding for some reason, and what better place to hide out than with her mother. We drove over there, but no one answered the door. We're going to try again if Patti doesn't turn up."

"Why don't I go with you instead? If Patti's there, she might not be happy to see Walt, especially if he's the one she's hiding from."

Elizabeth grinned. "I hadn't thought of that. Or is it you're trying to limit my time with Walt?" She let out a soft laugh, and said, "That's fine. You might have a point. And from Walt's point of view, I don't believe he'd be happy to find out she's been okay the whole time, while the cops have him on the spot for harming her."

"When do you want to go?"

"During my afternoon break tomorrow," she said. "Might as well do it and get it over with. So what's your plan? Knock on the door and ask if her daughter's there?"

"Something simple like that. The straightforward approach works best. If she's not with her mother, I might have some other ideas. Tell me more about what you know."

"Let's see. Walt doesn't seem to know much about her. I never understand people like her. By the time I've spent a few hours with someone, I've told them where I was born, my parents, my siblings, my jobs, my education, and maybe what I ate for breakfast. How can you have a conversation with someone and never talk about yourself?"

"Maybe, she keeps talking about other things so much so that there isn't an opportunity to get deep enough to reach beneath the surface for personal details. I do that at company receptions. Meetings with strangers require lots of meaningless chitchat to establish an artificial bond with someone with the principle aim to use the connection for a future purpose. After talking golf, politics, and the general business landscape, you don't know anything more about the details of their lives than when you started. On the other side, you have a whole different breed of cat—people with something to hide that make an art form out of deflecting personal questions."

"I guess you're right. He said she insisted on going to lectures at ASU about art history and archeology, and to functions at the Phoenix Art Museum." She flushed remembering that she met Walt at the museum. "He said she kept their conversations on those subjects. She never gave him a clear answer about her job, either. Maybe she has plenty of money or has a pension."

"Or she could be a criminal," Edgar said.

"I guess anything's possible." Elizabeth said. She frowned at him and wondered if he would be helpful after all.

"Tell me about Walt. What type is he?"

"What do you mean, type?"

"Like, is he a drinker? Is he a sports fanatic? Is he gambler? What does he do for fun? What does he do for work?"

"Oh, I see. Well, he's a contractor, self-employed. He likes art, but he's more the sports fan, football and basketball. We used to go to the Diamondbacks and Cardinals games here in town. He's tends to be a loner with his family in Kentucky. I don't think he realized how different Phoenix can be from the small Midwest towns he's used to."

"Why don't we call him to find out if there've been any developments?"

"Yeah, okay," she said. She pulled out her phone, scrolled, and started the call. She saw a questioning look on Edgar's face, no doubt wondering why Walt was still in her contacts list. "I keep everyone in my phone. I don't want to be caught off guard if a number comes up that I don't remember. That way I don't answer if it's someone I don't want to talk to."

"Don't look so guilty," he said, but she heard the jealous tension in his voice.

Walt answered. Elizabeth wanted to steer the conversation to the neutral subject about Patti right away. "Walt, it's Elizabeth. I have good news. A friend of mine wants to help. He's offered to hire a private investigator to do a background check on Patti. That might turn up a clue about where she might be."

"He must be a really good friend. That's not cheap."

"Yes, he is," Elizabeth said. "He's here with me right now and suggested I call you to make sure we have everything you know about her."

"I guess I should be flattered you're calling me while you're on a date."

"Funny, that's what you are." She hoped Walt understood she was trying to keep their conversation business-like and impersonal. She also hoped Edgar did not.

"I told you everything I know about her today. This thing's been weighing on my mind. I can't think of anything else. I hope you and your friend come up with something. Thanks, and thank him for me."

"You're welcome. I will. Try not to think about it. Call the lawyer tomorrow. Talk to you when we learn something."

Elizabeth looked over to Edgar. "Satisfied?"

"What do you mean?"

"You wanted to hear in my tone if you could detect intimacy between us. You're wondering if there's still something going on."

"Am I that transparent?"

"Yes," Elizabeth said.

"I guess I don't have any right to be jealous.

"No, you don't. Besides, I wouldn't turn him away even if you were."

Edgar kept his eyes on her until she became uncomfortable. "What?"

"It occurs to me that you're not as timid as you used to be. I can see I'm going to need to work harder than I expected to get you back."

Elizabeth could not hold back a laugh. She would not admit this to him, but her assertiveness had more to do with protecting her heart than confidence she might have developed over the years.

Friday Evening

When Walt called the police detectives working on the case to inquire about the status of the investigation, they were not forthcoming with developments. What they would tell him is that there were no new leads in the case. Walt's interpretation—we still think you did something to her.

Patti had been missing since last night. He knew she had planned for them to attend a lecture tonight at the university, so he decided to attend. She might have mentioned plans to go somewhere or talked about anyone that made her uncomfortable, but he had one problem with this plan. She mentioned her conversations with other committee members, but never their names. At least he knew two women by sight who sat with them once or twice. Even if they were not close with Patti, one of them might know someone who was. With all the time she said she spent there, she must have talked about other friends not involved in the academic world.

He recognized a slim, brown-haired woman sitting in the second row. Definitely, out of his league here or back home. Her coiffed hair looked stiff, but in place. With her tailored business suit, polished high heels, and powdered face, she looked too hot to handle and much too expensive to keep. When he sat in the empty chair next to her, she flinched. A flicker of resentment rushed over him at her implication.

"Excuse me. I believe you're a friend of Patti Slocum's. I wonder if I could ask you a few questions about her activities here. She's gone missing, and I'm trying to find her."

The woman seemed to study him with skepticism.

"I think I remember you," she said. "Yes, I know her, but not well. She attends the general meetings and volunteers sometimes. She's an acquaintance, but in no way would I describe her as a friend."

"Oh," Walt said. He did not usually make that distinction, but then that might be important for a woman like her. "That's disappointing. Is there anyone else here who might be close to her?"

"Not really. It's more as I described. We're all sociable here. We help out when we're needed, and we see one another at the functions. Some of us have established friendships outside of this group, but not too many of us are close. Like I said, we're sociable through our common interests. That's it."

Walt blew out his frustration. "Well, thank you for speaking to me."

"Certainly. Maybe we'll see you again."

She must be referring to the collective 'we," Walt thought. "Enjoy your evening, ma'am." If these women saw him again, it would not be here. The lecturer started to set up at the podium, so he left quickly. He had his fill of culture.

Walt got back in his truck and stared out the window. That had been a big waste of time, but confirmed what he kept uncovering. The people in Patti's life accepted her at face value. She had not allowed regular *acquaintances* close enough to ask the penetrating questions. Was she secretive and vague because she was a private person, or did she have another reason to keep her distance? Walt had become curious about this tiny woman with grand aspirations of remaking him. Although he considered their brief relationship over, he had not wished her harm. To the contrary, he was beginning to feel protective over her. She had become a sympathetic character— someone craving acceptance, yet keeping everyone at arm's length. He thought he understood that.

Speculating like this produced nothing. He decided on a different approach. He had to think hard about their conversations, focus on the times she let down her guard, and talked freely. Somewhere in their dialog, she must have dropped a clue about where she would go, or a problem that bothered her. Based on what he kept learning, he might have been the closest person in her life and the only one to figure out how to find her.

He closed his eyes and visualized walking through her front door the last time she invited him for dinner. She had a minimalist style, but she was not a fanatic about it. Her modern black and tan furniture seemed to stand at attention in the living room. He remembered small areas of organized clutter in various locations from an end table to the dining room table on the left. Nothing unusual there. She had been excited to show him the improvements she had made and guided him along on a tour. He strained his memory to recall her comments when they came up to each room. Most of what she said bored him and he had stopped listening. When they reached the basement, he remembered his surprise at her pride about an area that still looked unfinished.

She had looked at him with laughing eyes, and asked him what he thought of her designer basement. He had responded that it was nice, although he had not seen anything *designer* about it. A laundry room to one side, the partially finished basement had the usual metal shelves reserved for cleaning products and chemicals, paint and brushes, and yard and pool supplies. In one corner, a toilet inside a shower curtain for privacy, and a utility sink. All he saw was a barebones affair that under different circumstances, he would have suggested she have finished out for a family room or extra bedroom. She had said, "You just don't see it, do you?" He had answered that he did not—whatever *it* was. Without giving him an explanation, she led him back upstairs to their waiting dinner. He had written off the incident, but now the memory nagged at him that there might be something significant in the basement, if he could remember.

Saturday Morning

Elizabeth had trouble sleeping most of the night until she drifted off into an exhausted slumber around four. Walt and Edgar were chasing her to the edge of a cliff. Her choice to jump rather than to let either catch her startled her out of the dream and she opened her eyes. Her heart still pounded when she looked at the time. Just after eight. She thought about staying in bed longer, but her cell phone alerted her to two messages.

She had texts from both men inviting her to breakfast, but she answered that they should join her at her house and they could eat with her. She did not care that they resented one another's presence. After negotiating with herself about what to cook, she pulled out fresh fruit and milk, along with dry granola cereal and three bowls and plates. No fuss. She brewed an espresso for herself to have while she waited, and stared at the coffee mugs she set on the counter. The doorbell rang as she emptied her cup. Perfect timing.

"Good morning, guys. How'd you both manage to get here at the same time?

"Lucky, I guess," Edgar said.

Elizabeth thought Walt looked too amused at Edgar's irritation.

They walked into the kitchen where both men took a seat and looked up at her expectantly.

"This is a self-serve operation. There's fruit and granola cereal. The milk's in the fridge." From the looks on their faces, she could tell they expected something more substantial, but she moved unconcerned past them, filled her own bowl, and sat down.

Even after her jolt of caffeine, Elizabeth did not feel as alert as she thought she should, and the men looked as tired as she felt. Neither man had shaved, darkening their already worried faces. She understood Walt's weariness. Anxiety over Patti and the police hinting that he had something to do with that, anyone could understand, but Edgar's tension might be from having second thoughts about his adventure into the past. She laughed to herself how she had two men this morning, but could have neither tonight.

Both pairs of eyes focused on her when her laugh slipped out.

"I'm sorry, I was thinking about a dream I had." Anxious to

change the subject and redirect their focus elsewhere, she said, "Walt, have you heard anything new?"

"No, but last night, I tried to go over some things in my mind, and I'm curious about something she said about her basement." Walt recounted her comments about the basement.

When he had finished, Edgar perked up. "You said there were shelves along the wall?"

"Yes, the usual metal shelves with adjustable metal framing."

"Have you ever heard of a safe room?"

"You mean like the one in the Jodi Foster movie," Elizabeth said.

"Exactly,' Edgar said.

"Sure, I've heard of them," Walt said. "I've even helped build a couple before. You think Patti has one?"

"That would explain her comments and lack of explanation. Owners are supposed to be secretive, the whole point being that no one on the outside knows of it so if they need to hide, they can slip into safety until the police arrive. The rooms have wires linking the alarm system directly to a security company, sometimes by a landline. What if she's in there, but something happened to prevent her from communicating?"

Elizabeth jumped up and reached for the phone. "I'm calling the police to tell them. I bet they would know how to find out if she has one or not. My God, what if she's been in a room like that all of this time?"

"Wait a minute," Edgar said. "Let's try her mother's place first. We don't want to have the police tearing through the house and find out later she was staying with her mom. If she's the litigious type, she could hold us responsible."

"Maybe you're right," she said. "Walt, what do you think?"

"Might as well. I can't believe she misled me about her mother," Walt said. "It's the type of thing makes you wonder if you know a person at all. I'm sorry for her, but she's not the person I thought she was. Yes, she could be there. Maybe she's hiding with the idea of creating a mystery. You know, for attention."

"I hope not, for her sake. I'd hate to think of what I'd say to her," Elizabeth said. "Okay, here's what I suggest we do. Walt, since you know about construction permits, can you find out if someone applied for one for the basement?"

"That's easy. I can look on the *Permit Information Search* on the City of Phoenix Development website to find out any issued for that address."

She turned to Edgar. He looked disappointed staring down into his cereal bowl. "You said your detective was fast. Maybe he'll have something on her by now. I have to get into work for the lunch crowd. Can you pick me up at two? We'll go straight over to meet Madame Verna Kilgore."

"That sounds good. I can get some breakfast and catch up on the newspapers while I wait."

"Didn't like my breakfast, I guess," Elizabeth said.

"Sorry, but no. Breakfast is an important meal. I need protein, not carbs and sugars. No problem, though. I'm a big boy. I can take care of myself."

"Good to hear. Okay. I need to kick you both out so I can get ready for work. Walt, I'll call you as soon as we leave Verna's."

She ushered them out and shut the front door behind them. She leaned against it, rolled her eyes, and snickered.

The busy lunch crowd kept her too busy to think about much more than the immediate needs of the patrons and staff. When she finally caught her breath, she looked at the wall clock and read one-thirty. She changed into jeans and a t-shirt, touched up her makeup, and pulled her hair back into a loose ponytail. She checked her desk for any task she might have overlooked before heading toward the front. Edgar had arrived and waited for her at the bar.

"Hi," Elizabeth said. "Get enough to eat at the hotel?"

"Yes, plenty. Let's do this. I'll be glad to get this mystery solved."

"You sound like you're not having a good time in

Phoenix."

"Phoenix isn't the problem."

Elizabeth decided to let him stew for a while. She had not made up her mind about him—his return, his wife, and all the curious details he had not told her yet. "Here's the address. She lives close, in south Scottsdale."

Edgar moved the car into traffic. They were in front of the small house inside of twenty minutes. It stood quiet and unchanged from the first time she'd seen it. No detectable movements or audible sounds, like kitchen noise or a television. While Elizabeth peeked around the side of the house, Edgar rang the doorbell. She joined him on the front stoop, straining to hear any sign of life.

"I'm nervous all of a sudden," Elizabeth said. "Dropping in unannounced on one stranger to ask personal questions about another stranger sounds crazy. Maybe we shouldn't do this. Maybe Walt should be here instead."

"Relax. It's not an everyday thing, but we're not doing anything wrong. I'm glad you didn't try this on your own, though." He pressed the bell again. They both held their breath when the door started to open. A small nose poked out from the dark space behind the half-opened door. "Who's there?"

"Ms. Kilgore, my name is Elizabeth Kearn. This is my friend, Edgar Hamilton. We're here about your daughter."

"Abby's not here."

Elizabeth blinked. Does she have two daughters? "We're not looking for Abby. It's Patti who seems to be missing. She hasn't been seen in a couple days. The police are concerned as well."

"The *police*? Oh for crying out loud. What's that girl been up to now?" She loosened her grip on the door and let it swing open. "I guess you should come in."

"Thank you," Elizabeth said. When she saw the older version of Patti, she staggered backward from fright. This woman had the same features, but coarse wrinkles amplified the negative spaces of her face. Edgar walked behind her into the house. An overwhelming stench of ashes and stale cigarette butts struck her nose. "We won't stay long."

"Patti disappeared Thursday night, and no one's seen or heard from her since," Edgar said. "We wondered if she might be here. We're concerned she's been hurt, and that's why she's out of touch."

"Well, first off, I only have one daughter and her name ain't Patti. It's Abigail, Abby for short. And she's not here. As for someone wanting to harm her, I can't think of anyone. That wacko family she married into still live in California, far as I know. That's why she moved here. To get away from them."

Elizabeth noted that Verna had not invited them to sit, but when she looked around the small living room, she decided that was because she had no available seating anyway. Her creepy dolls and stuffed animals lined up on every available surface like friends attending a party. They took up the sofa and two club chairs. A recliner had a clear space that she presumed Verna saved for herself. Elizabeth turned back for a better view of her. Verna's head tilted and her eyes went out of focus. She looked confused, reminding Elizabeth of her grandmother's expression, *slightly cracked*. The more she looked around the place, the more she thought that was a fitting description.

"Do you have the name of her friends? You know anyone she might have gone to visit?"

"She ain't got no friends. All she does all damn day is screw around with them library books. Who cares what happened in the past, I keep saying? I told her she was wasting her time with education. She should get out and find another husband. Hell, I've been married five times. That don't mean I'm done." Verna winked at Edgar.

Elizabeth pressed her lips together to suppress a laugh, and avoided Edgar's eyes. When he did not respond, she said, "Anything unusual happen with her the last couple of weeks that might be important in retrospect?"

"Now you mention it, there's one thing." Verna leaned her face forward in an earnest expression, placed her hand on Elizabeth's forearm, and said, "Somebody stole my underwear."

"What?" Edgar said.

Elizabeth prayed he did not turn toward her. She reached over to covertly squeeze him arm. *Please don't look at me, or I'll crack up.*

"Just what I said, someone stole my underwear," Verna went on. "I went to look for my skimpy knickers, but all I found were these granny panties." She pulled inside the waist of her slacks to expose the elastic band of her white cotton panties. "This is all I have left. It's bad enough when you learn Madonna stole your only song. I told Patti something like this would happen by having that spy contraption sitting right in the living room." Verna pointed at the flat-screen television hanging on the wall.

Elizabeth had no idea how she kept a straight face, but she inhaled and said, "When did you see your other underwear last? Maybe Abigail borrowed them."

"Just the other day, and I haven't seen Abigail. Besides, why would she? Maybe someone took them as a souvenir. Come in here. I'll show you."

Elizabeth still had not looked at Edgar when she followed Verna through a short hallway and into a bedroom. She recognized a hoarding problem as soon as she looked past the threshold. Clothes and shoes stacked higher than the wardrobe they leaned against. Empty picture frames, baskets, rolls of gift-wrap paper, a couple of lamps took up the floor around the perimeter of the room. Her bed half-buried under blankets, sheets, and pillows. Elizabeth could not figure out how anyone could find anything in here with all the junk.

"It's a little cluttered," Verna said. "I'll get around to straightening up one of these days. Here," she said. She moved to a chest of drawers covered with a blanket. "I kept them in here, but now the drawer's empty."

Elizabeth looked around and saw a laundry basket stuffed in the corner packed with clothes. "Wow, that's a shame," Elizabeth said. "Who's been in here to have the opportunity to steal anything?"

"Don't know. It's a mystery." Verna stood with her hands on her hips, looking too amused, Elizabeth thought.

"When we find Patti, I mean Abigail, she'll be able to help you find them for you." She turned to head back to the living room. Verna followed so close behind, a rush of freaky fear ran up Elizabeth's back.

"That girl of mine is a real disappointment. Always too easy at the wrong time. As soon as I saw her developing, I said, 'When those boys try to get in your pants, you tell 'em you already got one asshole down there.' But did she ever listen? No. Screwing around with every loser she met, and not one of them asked her to marry him. Why would they? That is until that Cyril. All he wanted was a substitute for the ex, a glorified babysitter."

Elizabeth stood next to Edgar again. She could not decide whether to be shocked, amused, or frightened. One thing she knew was she wanted to laugh, but dared not burst out in a fit of hysterics. Verna seemed like someone performing a character part in a bizarre cult film—living out weird fantasies in this tiny space, choking down cigarette smoke, and probably having long talks with the creepy dolls. What Verna did not appear to be was harmless.

"I'm sorry we can't help you with your problems, but we'll be sure to pass this on to your daughter when we catch up with her. It's been nice to meet you."

Edgar opened the door, they backed out, and pull it closed behind them. Neither said anything until they were in the car.

"God almighty," Edgar said. "I'm not surprised Patti didn't tell Walt her mother lived in town. I can understand her pretending to be someone *not* related to that fruitcake."

Elizabeth could not hold back any longer. She started laughing, holding on to Edgar's arm, shaking all over her body.

"I kept praying you wouldn't look at me. I knew if our eyes met, I'd start laughing, and wouldn't be able to stop." She noted that Edgar did not laugh. "No appreciation for the humorous side of life?"

"What's not funny is how bad we smell. That place was

disgusting."

"It's worse in the back. I'm sure I smelled a urine odor, too."

Still laughing, Elizabeth said, "My favorite was how Madonna stole her song through the television." The fact that Edgar kept a straight face made her laugh harder.

"I'm going to drop you off at home so you can get cleaned up. I need to get a shower and some clean clothes before I throw up. I hope I don't have to burn my good suit. Damn."

"I had the same idea. Too bad my clothes aren't white, or they'd get a soaking in bleach. She sure was foul." Elizabeth had calmed down, wiping tears from her eyes. She thought Edgar's dry attitude through this was comical, too. People who take themselves too seriously had become the butt of her jokes before.

They both hesitated when Edgar stopped the car in front of her place.

"I have to get back to work, anyway," Elizabeth said. "Come down after you clean up. We'll have dinner." She slammed the car door behind her and hurried up the walkway.

As soon as she walked into her house, she peeled off her clothes faster than she thought she ever had for a man. She turned on the shower and stepped inside the stall thinking only of getting clean. She stuck her head under the spray, but had to jump away from the cold water. Once the shower started to fill the room with steam, she eased under the lukewarm stream and lathered up her hair first. She watched the sudsy water run along her body and down the drain. The foul smell grew stronger before it washed away with the lather. She surprised herself at how much she pitied Patti at this moment.

Restored and refreshed, she called Walt to find out if he learned anything about a permit.

"Yes, I did. She had a contractor build it. The process got complicated, and they had to have the inspector out a few times."

"Great. Now we know where she *could* be. That's the only thing that makes sense."

"How about your meeting with her mother? How'd that go?"

Elizabeth hesitated.

"What? Is the news that bad?"

"It's not that. It's, well, her mother is not what any of us would've expected. She's a bit off-the-latch, a real nut."

"I didn't expect to hear that. What's nuts about her?"

"Where do I start? First, the small house reeks of rotten food, cigarette smoke, and urine. She's like a crazy cat lady, but she collects dolls instead. They're all over the front room, taking up all the seating. Then, she's a terrible hoarder. The dolls and the hoarding aren't so bad, but I'm pretty sure she's delusional. She thinks Madonna stole her song through the television. And she insists someone stole her underwear."

"You mean out of the dryer?"

"I think she believes someone came into her home and exchanged her sexy underwear for high-waisted cotton briefs. You know the kind they call granny panties. I guess you had to be there for the full effect. I understand why Patti didn't tell you about her mother. I'd be embarrassed too. I kind of feel sorry for Patti. No wonder she wants to lose herself in art. What a burden to have a mother like that."

Walt did not speak right away. Elizabeth imagined him turning over this new information in his mind to form a new understanding of Patti's character. Even though he said their relationship was over, she suspected he still had feelings for her that brought out the masculine reaction to rescue and protect a woman in peril.

"I don't know what to say. She built up a grand résumé of her mother's accomplishments. I'm shocked."

"There's more. Verna claims she has only one daughter, named Abigail."

"Do you think that's part of her delusions or fact?"

"That's a good point," Elizabeth said. "Then again, she could be lying to protect Patti from strangers tracking her down."

"So now the question is whether Patti has a sister," Walt

said. "If she does, that would explain the name on the deed on her house."

"Gosh, I hadn't made that connection yet. You're right. A sister makes so much sense. So we can assume that Patti's with her sister and Verna lied about having only one daughter. That's cleared up that mystery thanks to Verna, crazy or not. So here's the thing. Let's call Detective Macy and let him know about the sister and Patti's safe room. I'll be on the line with you."

"I'm ready for this to be over. Let's do it."

Elizabeth heard the weariness in his voice, and wanted the same. She dialed the number he gave her, and once she connected, she brought Walt in to the conference call.

"Detective Macy, my name is Elizabeth Kearn, a friend of Walt Perry's. I'm here with him now. We have information on Patti Slocum's disappearance."

"Hi, Ms. Kearn. What have you got for us?"

"Walt, do you want to tell him about the safe room, or shall I?"

"Go ahead," Walt said.

Detective Macy was silent as Elizabeth told him what they learned about Patti's basement.

"That's interesting," Macy said. "We didn't look for that when we went through her house. Very clever of you both."

"I've had experience with safe rooms at other homes," Walt said. "I might be able to find it now that I know. From the way she talked, I think it's behind the metal shelves."

"Detective Macy paused, and then said "Okay. I'll meet you over there in an hour. Don't go inside on your own."

When they disconnected, she called Edgar to ask him to pick her up on the way to Patti's house.

"I'll be right over."

When she slipped into the passenger seat, Elizabeth thought Edgar looked tired. Or was that discouragement? Meeting Patti's mother was enough to depress anyone, but he might not be happy to have his visit to Phoenix interrupted by amateur sleuthing—especially on behalf of an ex-lover.

When they arrived, Elizabeth remembered the search she had done on the home's owner. In all the excitement, she had forgotten to mention it to the detective until she saw the officers in Patti's front driveway. When she identified Detective Macy, she rushed over to tell him.

"Detective, I looked up the property on the assessor's website and I found out this house belongs to someone named Abigail Bradley. From speaking with her mother, I think Patti Slocum and Abigail Bradley are sisters."

"The public must have the idea we don't have the same access to the web that they do, but thanks for trying to help."

"Well, don't you find it suspicious that Patti says this is her home?"

Detective Macy gave her a patient look. "We're aware of the situation."

Deflated, Elizabeth stood to the side while Detective Macy and the officers entered the house. They had been able to get inside after her initial disappearance by locating a spare key under a rock by the back door. Motioning Walt to follow them, Elizabeth and Edgar followed but kept their distance. As they started down into the basement from the kitchen, the sudden illumination from the overhead light blinded them until their eyes adjusted. At the bottom of the stairs, Walt pointed to the shelves. Working side by side, Walt, the detective and the two officers felt around the back of the shelves until someone said, "Found it."

"It's probably sound proof. At least they're supposed to be," Walt said.

"This is going to be quite a job to open this door if we don't find the emergency switch," another officer said.

Edgar pressed between the four men, and reached underneath the shelves one at a time until he found a tiny button all but unnoticeable, only detectable as an incongruous raised area on an otherwise flat metal surface. Nodding to the detective, Edgar moved back, and explained. "I've known people with these rooms before. There has to be a mechanical override to the system, and they often use the shelving system like this."

The detective and the officers pushed the three back into the opposite corner and drew their weapons. Elizabeth went cold anticipating the worst.

"What are you doing?" Walt's voice grew panicky.

"We have to take precautions. Folks that barricade themselves in these rooms often are armed and terrified. If she cannot hear us, she could think we're the ones she's hiding from in the first place. We're not going to just shoot her," Macy said.

Macy pressed the button. Everyone seemed to draw breath and freeze. A door began to appear out of the wall and started to move toward them.

"Ma'am, we're the police. There's no need to be afraid."

Elizabeth saw the tension release in Walt's shoulders the instant they heard the small voice respond with, "Okay."

Eventually, the door revealed the inside of the room. Everyone fixed their eyes on the scene as more came into view. Elizabeth remembered this feeling as a child, waiting to see if her fantasies would come to life by holding a stare long enough. When the door stopped moving, the officers' guns still drawn, Patti walked out of the room looking bewildered and frightened. When she saw Walt, she ran to him, slammed her body into his, and wrapped her arms around his neck, sobbing and muttering.

Everyone in the room relaxed. No danger. The lost is found. A good day for everyone.

"I've been so afraid. I didn't know if I should come out or not. I thought *he* might still be here."

Patti seemed to subrogate her control to Walt. Her body shook violently with the outpouring of tears. Elizabeth wondered if Patti *was* all right. The tension of hiding in an underground room with no outside contact for days had that effect. Walt held her to keep her calm. Elizabeth heard the officers requesting the paramedics and thought this a good time for her and Edgar to leave.

She nudged him and turned to head back up the stairs.

When she swung around, she bumped into a coat rack. It swayed dangerously side to side. She grabbed hold of the wooden stem to steady it, but then something red caught her attention. She looked with no particular interest until she saw the dried red paint that had dripped down the side of a can. Red paint? No way. Could Patti be her attacker? This was not the time to throw around accusations in her condition. The woman had given her the creeps that night, but surely, this was nothing more than a disturbing coincidence.

She wanted to say goodbye and tell Walt they were leaving, but he had not turned back toward either of them once he had taken charge of Patti. He wrapped her in one of her own blankets from the room and caressed her hair to sooth her. They checked with the officers to find out if they needed anything from either of them, and got the okay to leave. They got into Edgar's car and drove away.

"Thank God that's over," Edgar said.

"Yeah," Elizabeth said. "Me too." But she could not shake the alarm of seeing the red paint can.

Saturday Late Afternoon

Walt rode with Patti in the ambulance on the way to the hospital. The paramedics gave her a mild sedative for shock that also stopped her trembling. Walt barely recognized her, now fragile and out of control. She whimpered, squeezing his hand, begging him not to leave her. She closed her eyes, and he thought she had settled down until her lids began to move in rapid movements of mock violence during sleep. He had never seen anyone in this state before and could not understand this strange phenomenon. She woke up, or came to, and her body fell back on the stretcher more comfortably. When she relaxed, he started to move his hand away, but she kept a strong grip.

"Please don't leave me."

"I'm not going anywhere. I'm right here with you. Some doctors at the hospital are going to check you out and make sure you're okay."

She seemed relieved. She breathed in and out in jagged puffs, and said, "Good."

When she spoke to the police after they found her, she had not said much of anything toward explanation, only that she was afraid for her life, and begged them to protect her.

Detective Macy had been kind, but insistent. "Ms. Slocum, do you have any idea who could have sent you the notes or know of any motive for someone to do so?"

She screamed, "That's your job to find out! If I knew I'd tell you!"

Macy gave her an intolerant look. "I'll speak to you later when you're more responsive."

Knowing Patti as he did, inflexible and overbearing, Walt had no idea how to help her except to sit beside her and hold her hand. He looked over at her pale face and quivering lips. In one sense, she looked like a timid child, but a nagging thought kept nudging him that she might have staged this as a ploy for his attention. But would someone with her ego really risk it? Someone with so much pride, she would lie about her own mother?

Once they arrived at the hospital emergency room Walt tried to stay close, but the paramedics had called ahead and took her directly to triage for assessment. He stayed in the inner waiting room in the treatment zone to wait for news.

This hospital, a high-volume trauma center, buzzed with activity. Dreary places in the best of times, emergency facilities reminded him that the human body was easily broken. A man had been stabbed, another shot, a woman rushed in with an unconscious infant in her arms.

Amid the deafening noise of suffering patients and the chaos from inside the ward heard between the intermittent opening of the swinging doors that lead to the beds, he expected to see the usual child with a sprained ankle or viral illness. Children were conspicuously absent. The patients here represented a slice of big city life he wanted to avoid so that he could pretend did not exist. Just like everyone else, he supposed. The rancid odor of body grime, cigarettes, and fermented alcohol breath made him want to escape outside for fresh air, but he waited inside with everyone else.

When asked about her condition, a nurse had told him she had been taken to an examining room, and the doctor would be with her shortly. He wanted to lie about their relationship but thought better of it. After sitting there for over two hours, a nurse he had not seen before motioned him to follow her. She pointed him to Patti's makeshift room walled only by a hanging curtain.

"Welcome, Mr. Perry. Your young lady is a little dehydrated and shook up, but nothing serious. She's been sedated, but she'll be fine after a good rest." Patti looked inquiringly at the doctor standing over her. "Since you'll be with her, she can go home tonight. You'll need to watch her to make sure she doesn't stumble and fall, but when the drugs wear off, she'll be as good as new. A police officer is close by waiting to interview her, but he might be out of luck tonight."

"Oh, is there?" Walt said. "No one told me. That's good, I guess."

When they left the hospital an hour later, Walt doubted he did the right thing by assuming the responsibility to take her home. Her head dropped forward like a ragdoll's, and she had trouble answering simple questions. He had hoped to convince her to tell him the truth, but that was impossible right now.

He wanted to make sense of what had happened the last few days. After worrying over the unwelcome police attention, enlisting Elizabeth's help, as well as Edgar's, he was not happy to learn she lied about owning her house. Another invention. She distinctly had given him reason to believe she purchased the property. Why would she spend the money to build a safe room in a home that was not hers anyway? At least, she told him she paid for it. Now he wondered if the real owner had made the improvements before she moved in there.

His resentment started festering about the lies she told him about her mother. Walt guessed he understood why anyone would feel shame from the description Elizabeth gave him of the woman, but who really cared about that kind of thing these days? Almost every family he knew had at least one eccentric relative. They were only dating, for heaven's sake. Why mention her mother at all?

Those lies were bad enough, but he had other gnawing suspicions about other things. Could this drama be related to her past? He doubted she would be honest if he asked, even under sedation. Once she was lucid, he was convinced she would be more inclined to shut down and refuse to talk if he confronted her.

He carried her into the house and propped her against the pillows piled on her bed. Convenient that she had not made the bed. As a rule, men were more practical in that type of thing. He held back a laugh when she started moving her head around. All he could think of was a Patti bobble-head.

"What's going on here?" she said. "Who's in my house? Don't forget to set the alarm. Thirsty. I need a drink." She started to stand but leaned forward almost going down headfirst until he caught her. "Unhand me! I command you!"

"Oh, shit," Walt said. *She's a mess. How am I going to handle her in this state?* "Patti, it's Walt. I brought you home from the hospital. I'm trying to take care of you."

"Walt, it's you?" She squinted at him. "Thank God, you're here."

"Lie back and relax. The doctor gave you some sort of tranquilizer, so you need to be careful about falling. Are you hungry?"

"No, but I'm thirsty."

Now he had to decide if he could leave the room without her trying to get up on her own. "Tell me what you want, and I'll get it if you promise not to move."

"Okay. Promise."

Walt did not believe her, but he had no choice. He was thirsty, too. And hungry. He had forgotten to eat lunch and dinner. He rushed downstairs, grabbed a bottled water, a straw, and a glass of milk, and rushed back to her. She had not moved. Good. He held the bottle and guided the straw for her to drink. She drank half of it before holding up her hand to stop.

He flipped on the television, put the volume on low, and took a seat to drink his milk.

"Feeling better?"

"Yes, but I can't seem to focus very well."

"That's the drugs. The doctor said that feeling will wear off once you sleep it off."

He watched for signs she had fallen asleep. He had to have more than a glass of milk. When he heard her gentle snoring, he tiptoed out of the room and back downstairs. He peeked outside as he crossed through the living room. A patrol car sat imposingly in the front of the property. Walt waved and went back to the kitchen. When he checked the refrigerator and found so many leftovers, he could not believe his luck. He heated up raviolis, a pork chop, and a slice of apple pie, and hurried back to Patti's room. He did not think she had not moved. Now he could relax.

He ate, finished his milk, and then raised the footrest of the recliner to watch a movie. He still has so many contradictory feelings about her. He looked over at her sleeping. Maybe he was more of a fool than he knew, because he started to have second thoughts about dumping her. So what if she put on airs. Insecure people did that. Maybe he had been wrong to suspect she manipulated recent events for some bigger reason. Her gentle expression gave her a vulnerability that spoke to his nature to shield her from harm.

He leaned back, and wanted to close his eyes. A surprising tiredness took over. After today's excitement and the heavy meal he had eaten, he needed a nap. Now that she had fallen sound asleep, he figured he could take a quick nap, but be alert enough to wake up if she needed him. Before he had time to turn off the television, he fell asleep.

Saturday Evening

With Walt out of his hair and occupied with Patti, Edgar knew the rest of this day had to get better. He looked forward to being alone with Elizabeth without distractions.

He regarded her as she leaned back in the car seat, her drowsy eyes almost closed. Even disheveled and exhausted, she still had that same natural beauty he remembered. Maybe her unaffected nature made her beautiful. Coming here had been the right choice. From what he saw so far, her life here was tentative—in a holding pattern waiting for something important to happen, her relationships inconsequential, her job trivial and mundane. At least that was how he saw her.

"What drama, ay?" Edgar said.

"I'm stunned," Elizabeth said, opening her eyes as she roused from her catnap.

"I don't think you can get a better climactic moment from anything you watch on television. But seriously, do you really think someone threatened her and wants her dead?"

Elizabeth hesitated. "Well, I heard her tell the police she'd received two threatening letters. She said she saved them. All I can do is *assume* she's in danger like she said. I told the detective about how her house was in someone else's name, but he said he already knew about that. I bet this confusion between Abigail Bradley and Patti Slocum is related."

"True. I agree that something seems wrong. The picture doesn't hang straight."

Elizabeth looked thoughtful for a several seconds. "You're right. When I saw her at the restaurant the first time, she didn't strike me as the easily intimidated type. More like an aggressive menacing pit bill. Then, we watched that safe room door open, and she came out like a frightened rabbit, hysterical and weak, like a performance. I don't know what we can do about it though."

"The whole thing is none of our business. Never was," Edgar said. "You were helping out a friend, and I was helping you. Now that's over, and we can get on with our lives. I don't want to be callous, but I made this trip to be with you, not to spend time with strangers."

"I see your point. Let's do something fun."

"You don't need to go back to work?"

"Yes, I do, but I can take time to eat if I'm already there. I'm starving."

"You're not starving, unless you feel undernourished from that so-called breakfast."

"I guess I can count on not hearing the end of that for a while."

"Alright, I've made my point."

Edgar drove them to the Matrix. Elizabeth seated them herself, and then went to the bar to order drinks and check on the staff. He watched her posture in the restaurant, going from the kitchen, to the bar, to the front reception area. Her mastery of the restaurant operations impressed him. He thought, with some discomfort, how he paid so little attention to the people who worked in restaurants unless something happened he did not like. He tended to take a patronizing attitude toward waiters, servers, hostesses, and even the managers. Being here as practically a guest, getting this different perspective of all that was involved in a well-run establishment convinced him he need to make an adjustment to his superior attitude.

"Okay." Elizabeth returned and slid into the booth opposite him. "Our server will be right over with the drinks. I ordered you what you used to like. I hope you haven't gone off the taste of Chivas on ice?"

"No, I haven't. I'm surprised you remember."

A pretty server with a heart-shaped face, bright blue eyes lined with dark liner, and hair in a bun, set down their drinks, and looked at Elizabeth first.

"I'll have my usual, Tina."

Edgar looked at the menu and then at Tina. "I'll have the filet mignon medium rare, the squash instead of potatoes, mixed vegetables, with soup to start." He saw amusement in Tina's eyes, but ignored it. Girls in their early twenties tended to giggle and squeal a lot, finding humor in the oddest places that he could not comprehend.

He turned his attention on Elizabeth. "I'm impressed with this place."

"Thanks. I enjoy working here. We have a good crew right now. Makes it easy to come in to work." Elizabeth took a sip of water and looked away.

"Why the faraway look?"

"Just wondering again why you're here. Is it really me, or are you pining for the time when we knew each other. There's a big difference."

"I see where you're going with this, but that's not it. Sure, my life was simpler. I had goals and ambitions, still struggling to make my mark. The anxiety of not knowing if I would succeed, or if I'd have to come up with an alternate plan for my life. I don't miss those times. What I miss is your carefree spirit. Your sense of fun. Your generous nature toward other people."

"I'm probably a fool to consider taking you seriously. Men in mid-life crisis trying to recapture their youth. Fantasizing about younger days that can't ever return. Running back to the dependable wife at home who waits patiently while he gets this out of his system. Saying all that out loud sounds like a setup for another letdown."

Edgar flushed. Donna said almost those very words when he left. He started to open his mouth, but he saw Tina making her way toward them with their food. At least, he would have a chance to think of something to counter that.

Tina started to place the plates before them. She still had that smirk on her face, but now so did Elizabeth. She had uncharacteristically given him all his dishes before serving Elizabeth. He saw the humor when Tina served Elizabeth. She had ordered a bacon-double cheeseburger, chili fries, a Cesar salad, vegetable soup, and a small cup of fruit. The contrast between their food styles did look ridiculous, more as if he was having dinner with a ten-year-old instead of a grown woman.

"You two were waiting for my reaction," he said.

"I told Tina what I wanted while I was in the back. After your ribbing me about breakfast, I thought I'd have a little fun at your expense."

"Duly shocked. You're not really eating all that are you?" By the look on her face, it appeared she intended to eat every bite.

Edgar watched Elizabeth in astonishment at the volume of food she consumed. When she had soaked up the last of the fries in the chili, she asked Tina to bring her a blueberry cheesecake.

"I don't always eat like this," Elizabeth said. "But stress makes me hungry. After this afternoon, I needed comfort food. I'll be back on more religious fare tomorrow."

"Now that we've stuffed ourselves," Edgar said. "I have an answer to your earlier accusation. If getting a divorce is all it will take to convince you I'm serious, consider it done." He reached into his jacket pocket and pulled out his Blackberry, scrolled down the address list, pressed the trackball and listened. In less than a minute, he was telling his attorney the weather was beautiful in Phoenix, and he wanted to move forward with the divorce.

"Get the papers ready. I want to file as soon as I speak to Donna in person. I don't want to be a coward and drop this bomb on her while I'm away…Right…I'll talk to you next week." As he hung up, he looked at Elizabeth, "Do you believe me now?"

Elizabeth sniffed. "You could've been talking to your own voice mail for all I know. Listen, if you want to divorce your wife, fine, but don't do it on my account. If you're doing this because you believe you've got me lined up, don't. I'm not guaranteeing you anything. I don't want the pressure." Edgar gave her a wounded expression. "Can we just go now?"

"Do you want to go somewhere else?"

"No, I need to get some rest. We've had a full day. We're both exhausted, and I need some alone time before I go to sleep. Understand?"

"Sure, I do." He said the right words, but he did not mean

it. He thought about earlier when he believed the day would get better without Walt always present. Right now, he would prefer jealousy to rejection.

He pulled his car into her driveway, uncertain whether he should turn off the engine. Before he could reach over to kiss her, she opened the door and darted to her front entrance. She blew him a kiss and waved as she retreated into her home that she made obvious was off limits to him tonight.

Instead of driving away, he left the gear in park, hesitant to end their conversation this way. He remembered their exchange of words and wondered what he could have said to end the evening on a positive note. He had said it all wrong and needed another chance to explain himself. He could not let it stand this way.

He turned off the engine and stared at her house. It struck him as odd that she had not turned on the lights yet. The sun had gone below the horizon, so the natural light had lost its effect to illuminate the inside of a home enough to forego lighting. He strained his eyes to see her movement through the rooms, but everything remained motionless. Since he had already convinced himself he was going in to talk to her, he was half way up her walkway before he admitted something did not look right.

Once he moved closer to the front door, he saw she had left it ajar. She had always been clumsy and forgetful, but never placed herself in a dangerous situation. His heart pounded faster the closer he got to the doorway. He leaned into the darkness. The minimal light outside had enough brightness to cause a brief blinding effect as he strained to focus on the interior.

"Elizabeth?" Nothing but quiet. "Elizabeth," he said again. "Where are you? What's wrong?"

Finally, he heard movement at the back of the house and started toward the sound. He took a step but his foot caught on something in the middle of the floor. The momentum thrust him forward onto an ottoman. He turned to see what tripped him. The form looked large, like a big dog. Then, as his vision adjusted to the darkness, he saw the blonde hair and recognized the cotton jacket she wore this evening. "Oh, God. Elizabeth!"

Saturday Late Evening

Edgar knew he should have chased down the intruder, but he had to find out if Elizabeth was okay first. He fumbled around the room until he found a light switch. He flipped on the one closest to the door and watched the lamps illuminate the living room. He gasped when he looked at her. She looked worse than he imagined. Her head bled from under the previous wound, the small bandage covered in oozing red liquid. He vetoed the instinct to move her. He had to call the police and an ambulance.

Both vehicles pulled up at the same time. Edgar moved aside while the paramedics looked at her.

"Do you think this is related to the attack last week?" The officer taking his statement stopped to watch them.

"I wouldn't know. I arrived in town the next day. She told me about the first incident when I asked about her bandage. She talked as if she had no idea who would've done it, and I believe her. I wish I had more to tell you."

"Thank you, sir. That'll be all for right now."

Edgar moved back near Elizabeth who looked conscious now. The paramedics applied fresh bandages to her head, and kept saying something to her he could not hear.

"No, I don't want to go to the hospital again. I have a nasty headache, but I still have the pain meds from the other day."

"We really advise you to get checked out again. Second similar head injury in under a week."

"No, I'm fine. Really. I appreciate your concern."

Edgar walked toward her. "What if I drive you there?"

"No," Elizabeth said. "I'm not going, so everyone stop trying to bully me."

The two paramedics started putting their supplies away and packing up their equipment, but neither said anything else to Elizabeth. Edgar did not blame them. She could be forceful when provoked, he noticed. He stood away from the group, waiting for a good time to talk to her. *She is too independent for her own good.*

It did not seem long before all excitement had left the neighborhood. The emergency vehicle and police cars had gone. The neighbors went inside their houses. Elizabeth had gotten up and stretched out on the sofa. He sat in the chair near her.

"I bet Patti's mixed up in this somehow," Elizabeth said.

Edgar sat up straighter hearing her voice back to normal. "What do you mean?"

"I told you about how someone painted on my garage door and conked me in the head?"

"Of course, I remember,"

"Well, when we were in her basement, I saw a can of red paint that had previously been opened."

"Why would she do that?"

Elizabeth scrunched her face. "She's nuts for one thing. But I think she's jealous, as if she believes I want Walt back. I'll tell you, she looked like she could've killed me that night at the restaurant."

"Why didn't you tell the police when they interviewed you?"

"Because of all the drama and all the attention they've given her. They'd accuse me of making up the accusations out of some misguided spite."

"I'm not saying you're right or wrong, but tomorrow we'll find out where she was this evening. I assumed she would be in the hospital, but maybe not. Don't worry about it for now. Get some sleep. Rest up. I'm sleeping out here in case you change your mind about the hospital."

"You don't have to do that," she said. "I mean, you don't

have to stay here."

"I'm aware of that. But I'm staying. Period."

"Okay. Can you call Esme for me? She's in my contacts."

He scrolled down, found the number, and sent the call.

"Here," he said, handing her the phone.

She put the call on speaker, and said, "Esme, it's Elizabeth."

"You sound funny. What's wrong?"

"Someone hit me again," Elizabeth said. "In my own home. A second time. Can you believe it?"

"You're not alone, are you?"

"Edgar's here. He's going to stay the night to keep an eye on me." She looked up at his surprised face and winked.

"I've a couple of things to take care of then I'm catching a plane to Phoenix. I'll be there Monday at the latest. I'm worried about you."

"I sure would love to see you."

"Can Sir Galahad pick me up? I don't think you should try to drive. If not, I'll get a taxi."

"I'm sure he'd be happy to pick you up. Text me your flight number when you have it, and I'll pass it on." Elizabeth disconnected and set the phone on the coffee table. "You don't mind that I volunteered you, do you? I usually pick her up, and it's a short drive from here to the airport. I'll be glad to see her after all this craziness."

"Sir Galahad, huh? It's not how I'd choose to spend my morning, but I don't mind."

"Don't mind her. She likes to give everyone a nickname. Depends on her mood. Sometimes she calls me Miss Prissy Pants."

Edgar laughed. "I'm looking forward to seeing those soon, if you live long enough, that is."

Sunday Early Morning

Edgar woke to the sound of *Rondo a la Turca*, the current ring tone on his cell. He stretched his arm over the sofa arm to the end table and grabbed his phone from the charging cord. When he saw Sam's name flash across the screen, he pressed the answer button, and said, "Edgar Hamilton."

"Good morning, Edgar. Hope I didn't wake you. Sam Shelton here. I have news on that woman you called me about."

"Oh, she's been found. I guess it doesn't matter anymore, but you might as well tell me what you found."

"It was pretty easy. I would guess anyone could find out as long as they knew how. Most of this is public record. First, her real name was Abigail Slocum until she married Cyril Bradley about five years ago. That marriage only lasted a year. Before the divorce, there was a big stink about one of Cyril's daughters. The girl attacked Abigail and she pressed charges. Then, you know how the story goes. Both parents resent the outsider interfering, takes child's side, angry words spoken, threats made, marriage ends. As far as I could find out, Cyril practically ordered Abigail out of his house the same day she had the girl arrested. She left for London, Kentucky, and stayed with her mother for a year. She moved back to California, but the trouble started up again with the ex and the girl's mother. She moved to Phoenix about two years ago, and bought a house. No other trouble with the law."

"How does she earn a living?"

"She lives off an annuity from an accident she had several years ago."

"I see," Edgar said. "Anything else on the ex-husband? It seems excessive that he would still be angry after all this time."

"That's an interesting sidebar to the story. The entitled devil daughter couldn't keep her mouth shut and got into a fight with another girl while she was in detention. This other girl and her friends beat the crap out of her. Then, she had an unfortunate complication from the beating. When they took her to the infirmary to have the doctor check her out, he thought she had drugs in her system. She was dizzy, had trouble walking, slurred speech. Turned out she had a brain aneurysm. The violent blows to her head caused a rupture. She died within hours."

"God, that's awful."

Sam took a breath. "That's what everyone thought. The situation received a lot of press at the time. The parents tried to sue the city, but they lost. The mother yelled at the judge, accusing the justice system of murder. Of course, the girls who beat her up were charged with involuntary manslaughter, but the mother wanted more blood. What she wanted most was to see Abigail punished, saying that if she hadn't told the cops what happened, her daughter wouldn't have been there in the first place. Tragic business for everyone involved."

"That's terrible," Edgar said. "But if the girl already had the condition, wasn't it only a matter of time?"

"Grieving people don't always want to look at the obvious."

"So Abigail went to Kentucky?"

"Right. She tried to move back to California but that didn't last. Cyril found out, and began calling and leaving death threats. She recorded the calls and supplied them to the police. He was arrested, but served no time. She filed a protection order against the mother, but I think we all know how useless they can be against an obsessive person. That's when she moved to Phoenix and legally changed her first name to Patti and took back her maiden name. I don't think she realized property records are public and didn't change the deed on her home into her new legal name. Her mother has an address there."

"We met her. She's a real piece of work."

"By the way, I checked on Cyril and his ex-wife, Phyllis. Both have been out of touch the last two weeks. I don't know if they're together or not. The other two children are living with Cyril's parents, who said they expected him to be working out-of-state for his company. Might be legitimate, but he could've told that story to his parents to cover a trip here."

"Well, that's some juicy stuff. On this end, through a combined effort, we found Patti yesterday holed up in her safe room. She said she'd received death threats and feared for her life when she thought someone was in the house with her. She barricaded herself in and was then too afraid to come out. It was a hare-brained idea, if you ask me. It caused a lot of people a lot of trouble."

"What do you mean?"

"The police suspected her boyfriend of doing away with her. When he got worried they might arrest him, he asked Elizabeth for help. That's how I got involved. Once I saw that dumb-ass woman had been fine the whole time, I wanted to make her disappear all over again."

"I wondered what any of this had to do with you. I guess you don't want me to work on this anymore, then?"

"I don't see much point, do you? She's found, and Elizabeth's friend is no longer a suspect in her disappearance, so that should be the end of it for Elizabeth and me."

"Right. Should I mail my bill?"

"I'd prefer you email it like before. I'll take care of it personally. Thanks for getting on this so promptly. I appreciate it."

"I wish all my investigations were this easy," Sam said, and disconnected the call.

"Well now," Edgar said.

Sunday Morning

After days on the edge of panic, Patti opened her eyes expecting to be groggy from the escapades of the night before. Instead, she woke up alert and unusually peaceful. She smiled seeing Walt asleep in the recliner. She got out of bed, and looked out the window. A police cruiser passed by out front. She slid back in under the covers, and wrapped the comforter around her. As tentative as the current calm had to be, she savored Walt being here, watching over her, protecting her.

She still had a lot to consider. Sitting alone the past few days, she had come to realize the only people who hated her enough to stalk her were Cyril and his ex-wife Phyllis. She could look forward to living this nightmare wherever she moved until either she or both of them died. She had done all the rationalizing and beating herself up trying to think of some way she could have handled the situation differently. In the end, what happened, regardless of how tragic, could not be undone by harming her.

Through two years of therapy, she came to acknowledge only the part that might have been her fault. She had to get medical treatment that day. Sure, she could have lied about who attacked her, but she had answered mechanically when questioned, not as a person calculating future consequences. She could even accept blame for marrying Cyril in the first place. But no one could blame her for Maggie's attitude and the fight she started, or her medical condition no one knew the girl had.

Now she wanted to put all that behind her, but they would not leave her in peace. Would she ever get rid of them? Maybe Phoenix had been a bad choice with its easy accessibility to California. She could have stayed at her mom's place in London, Kentucky, but she could not take the harsh weather anymore. In hindsight, Florida would have been a better choice.

"Walt, are you awake?"

Walt could not believe he could not hear the effects of the sedation in her voice when she woke him up that morning. Instead, he thought she sounded more tired than someone with a drug hangover. He looked over at her, still propped up against her pillows as he had placed her the night before. Somehow, she had managed to find a comb and had smoothed out the hair around her face.

"You're feeling much better than yesterday," Walt said, and reached over to give her a platonic kiss at the side of her head.

"Yes, I'm much better. I didn't get the chance to thank you. I owe you a lot for the rescue, although I was surprised it was so easy to find my safe room. How did you figure that out?"

Walt sensed a hint of hostility directed at him. Ignore it.

"As I told the police, I've helped to install other safe rooms for clients in my construction business, and recognized some of the signs once I started to think on those lines. Besides, don't you remember your cryptic comments about the basement when you gave me the tour of your house? Giving me clues. I just put two and two together. Edgar is the one who found the emergency button."

"Who's Edgar?"

"A friend of Elizabeth's. I asked her for help when the police started looking at me as a suspect. He's visiting her from out of town. When he learned about it, he offered to help us find you."

"Oh," she said. "I see. Will you help me downstairs to the kitchen? Staying in bed makes me think I'm sick."

"Sure." He went over and helped her to her feet. "Are you dizzy?"

"No, I'm much more clearheaded than last night." She laughed. "I wonder what they gave me. I wouldn't mind having a little of that around the house for emergencies."

"I don't think that's a good idea. You were almost a vegetable."

"I was a vegetable when you found me. I must have been in some state when I walked out and saw all those people."

"That's true," he said.

"Listen, Walt. I need to explain some things from my past."

"Like what?"

"Like a marriage that went wrong. The reason I believe I'm being stalked and threatened."

"Let's talk about it over breakfast. I'm hungry." He wondered if she would tell him about her mother, at last.

Once he sat her on one of the chairs, Walt set sausage in a skillet, started a pot of coffee, and sat across from her. *Here's her chance.*

"We haven't known each other for too long so you don't know about my marriage. I'm divorced, and there were things that happened during that time that were... Let's just say it didn't go well. I don't like to talk about that period of my life. I'm embarrassed, humiliated even. You can't wake up from a nightmare like this. My therapist thought writing the story out would be therapeutic. I haven't been able to get started. Since all of the threats on my life, I need to look back and face it. I need to tell someone. I'm telling you because you're probably the person I'm closest to now.

"Let's have it."

"Cyril had three children—Amy, seven; Maggie, twelve; and Adam, fifteen. Though they were polite enough in the beginning, I must say Adam and Amy were always friendly and eventually grew to accept me. Maggie never did.

"She was a pretty girl who got a lot of attention. She also had a bad approach to life that attracted other kids with similar attitudes. Life handed her a bad hand, and she was going to make everyone suffer until she got a new deal.

"I guess it was bad enough that she had to put up with me, but then her mother started to date a man who travelled a lot. Cyril and I offered to keep the three kids all summer. Her new boyfriend had no children, so they were gone most of the time. I don't think he wanted them around, to be honest. But she called the kids from wherever they went to get personal updates on them. Her last call from Oceanside, California, came when Maggie and I were alone. Maggie had become agitated and slightly hysterical with her mother, demanding to know why she had been gone so long and why she couldn't stay home and take care of her. She accused her mother of not loving her anymore since that man came into her life. And she didn't leave me out. She talked about being stuck with me, while her dad abandoned her, too.

"By this time, Maggie looked apoplectic. Whatever her mother said had no calming effect on her. Then she started calling her mother a whore. After another five minutes of accusations, she slammed down the receiver into its cradle with such violence, I started to fear for my own safety. Cyril still hadn't come back. I half expected him to enter at the right moment, but he didn't. Where was he I needed him?

"When the child turned around, she looked inhuman. She lunged at me, grabbed me by the throat, and knocked me to the ground. The impact of my body on the Saltillo tile caused an excruciating sharp pain on my spine and jarred me breathless for at least a minute. She pinned me down and punched me in the face repeatedly. I used my arms to fend off her bony fists. Finally, I caught her wrists with both my hands, but I didn't have good leverage from my weakened vantage point. I could feel warm blood running from my nose into my left ear. No one had ever struck me in my entire life. I felt stunned and confused, but I wouldn't let go of her wrists.

"'Let go of me, you bitch,' she screamed.

"I screamed back, 'I'm not letting go so you can start hitting me again. Get off me and I'll think about it.' My anger gave me strength I didn't know I had. I squeezed until my nails pierced her skin. Apparently, feeling pain was not as enjoyable as inflicting it. She leaned off me sideways. That raised me up until we were standing opposite each other. She had calmed down, but still looked wild. When I released her wrists, she jumped back to check her arms, and then looked at me in disbelief.

"'Look what you've done. I hate you, you know.' She said. 'I've always hated you. If it weren't for you, my parents would have gotten back together. Now it's too late. I won't ever forget that. You're going to pay. All of you are going to pay for what you've done to me.'

"I didn't say a word. I didn't trust her for a second. I figured I could keep her at bay as long as she was not in a position to tower over me. She spit at me, ran to her room, and slammed the door.

"I couldn't stay there. I saw my purse near the front door with my car keys hanging out of the front pocket. I ran on tiptoes to the front door, picked up my purse, and left the house.

"It took me awhile to clear my head. I drove to a nearby park and washed my face with the emergency water I keep in the back of the car. The dried blood was not easy to remove, but after a good soaking with paper towels, I was able to wipe my face clean. Clearly, without the crud on my face, I had two black eyes. Then, I asked myself why I was hiding in a park at nine o'clock at night in fear for my life.

"I stopped trying to fix myself and drove to the emergency room at the closest hospital. They cleaned me up, took X-rays of my head and spine, and gave me a thorough examination. The doctor said I had no fractures, but minor contusions to the face and acute back sprain. They bound me into a corset-like thing that I had to wear for three weeks for my back and told me to apply an ice pack to my facial injuries twice a day.

"When the doctor asked who did this to me, I blurted out the whole story. I thought we were making conversation. Then he tells me the hospital's policy is to report assault cases to the police. I knew I'd be in for it about that, but I'd already told him everything.

"Once I started talking to a police officer, all my frustrations poured out—Maggie's attitude toward me, her mother's absence, Cyril's denial, how I suspected she and her friends were up to no good, and finally, the argument with her mother that incited the attack on me. I guess having someone to tell my story to spurred me on. I got angrier the more I talked. I was so riled up by the time I finished, I said I'd sign anything if that meant someone was finally going to do something."

"I woke up in the hospital the next morning almost not believing the day before happened. If not for the tightening around my torso from the corset, I would have thought I dreamed it all. I worried because I had not called Cyril. I reached over, grabbed the telephone, and dialed home.

"'Hello,' Cyril said.

"'Hi, it's me, Cyril. I need to talk to you to let you know what happened last night. I…'

"'Don't bother. I think it's obvious what happened here. You've got some kind of nerve calling me like this.' His taut voice was cold and threatening, and coming from the mouth of a man I did not know.

"'What do you mean? I'm the victim here. I'm the one who has two black eyes and has to wear a corset because of my back injury. Maggie could have killed me and you say I have nerve to call you? What kind of a man are you anyway?' My heart was pounding, and I felt violated from a place I least expected.

"'I don't care what she did. That was no excuse to have her arrested. This is a family matter, and it's not for you to call in the police and give her a police record. This could affect her whole life, and after what she's been through coming from a broken home, she doesn't deserve to go to court like a common criminal. I'll tell you something, you better be glad you're not here right now, because I'd give you something to hurt about, you no good, lying bitch.'

"The bum just hung up on me. I failed to see how any of this was my fault. My greatest shock was Cyril's attitude and lack of concern. I think that hurt me worse than the injuries.

"I had no further contact with that family after that day. I moved in with my mother in London for a year. When I went back to California, a former neighbor told me Maggie died in jail. I thought it was sad and unfortunate but nothing to do with me. Talk about a shock when Cyril saw me at a grocery store and came over, screaming at the top of his lungs that I had murdered his child, and that he would get even one day. I had to file a restraining order against him and his crazy ex-wife. That didn't help. I had no choice but to pack up and move.

"That's when I came here. I had to change my name and everything. I thought they wouldn't be able to find me. I guess I was wrong. You see that this wasn't my fault, don't you?"

Walt never said a word during her entire monologue. A couple of times, he thought he might throw up from his emotional mood swings her story caused. He had to keep his anger and irritation under control. She had a bad scare, and spilling her guts like this had to have a disturbing effect. If he did the right thing, he would make his own confession, but he decided this was not the right time.

"Do I sound awful? I hope you can understand how terrified I was to come home and find all my knifes and sharp objects missing, my car wouldn't start, I couldn't get my doors open."

Walt went to one of the kitchen drawers and pulled it out. Every imaginable knife, skewer, and cooking shears that someone could want were lined up nicely. "Are you sure about that?"

She got up and looked in the drawer. "I swear every drawer was empty.

"Okay," he said.

Patti looked distressed. "Don't you believe me?"

"Patti, everything's here. We arrived last night, and you were zoned out. Are you saying someone came here while we were out that evening, did all you say, and then put everything back before we found you?"

"That must be what happened. Don't you see that Cyril or Phyllis must be here in town? They're trying to terrorize me."

"For what happened to their daughter?"

"You don't think that was my fault? How could I have done anything differently?"

"I wasn't there, was I? Sure, I'm sorry you've had these problems, but don't ask me to take your side without question. After all, a child died."

"So, you think this was all my fault." Patti's expression went wooden except for the reddening on her cheeks.

Walt could see her holding back the tears. He looked at her with less sympathy than before. He had to get out of this house. "I've missed a lot of work the past week. I have to get back. Did you need anything else?"

"I guess not," said Patti. Her shoulders drooped. She looked defeated

Walt held up his hand in mock salute and left her without speaking. He should have just told her the truth—that he didn't want to see her anymore, for one thing. He had come up with plenty of excuses not to tell her, the best one being she had just been through an ordeal, but he knew the real reason was to avoid the confrontation. If necessary, he would tell her later. Maybe she would move away, and he would not have to admit anything.

Sunday Evening

After a day of sleeping off and on, Patti kept reliving the details of the scene with Walt, and trying to work out what happened. She had trouble figuring how she misjudged him. She stood in front of the mirror in her bathroom and studied her face as if she had never seen herself in in the light before. She shook her head. Nothing worked in her life. Was the answer in her face? She examined all of her features one at a time, then as a whole. What had she always heard? Do not look too closely at yourself in the mirror, because that is not how everyone sees you. From her tiny ski-slope nose, to the arch of her upper lip, her rosy cheeks, to her almond shaped eyes and finely arched brows, she found nothing distinctive. She looked like she could be anyone. So why could she not be someone else? Every time she tried to transform her life, the world threw her backward instead of propelling her forward. She sneered at the reflection of the hardened woman she found there.

She eased down into her bathtub full of steaming hot water and lavender bath salts. She rested back on her plastic tub pillow and prayed for this nightmare to be over. All in good time. Tonight, all she could do was be grateful to be back safe in her own bed. Tomorrow, she would decide what to do.

Monday Morning

The last thing Officer Hudgens expected when he drove past the Slocum house was a sleeping officer. Sure, they all knew how boring patrol could be, but to be sound asleep in his car was not acceptable. Officer Detwiler had not been on the force too long and seemed to lack understanding the importance of public opinion. What if this woman walked out and found him sleeping? What if she needed his assistance and was hurt because he could not wake up fast enough to help her?

"Rookies," he said, shaking his head. He tapped on the glass, but could not wake the young officer. Officer Hudgens started to have a bad feeling. Something did not feel right. He went from tapping with fingertips to pounding with the side of his fist. The window glass vibrated, but nothing roused the man inside.

An adrenalin rush surged through his body. He touched his gun, alert to his surroundings. He rushed to his own vehicle to call dispatch for backup to an officer in distress alert. He grabbed the door opener tool, rushed back to open the passenger side, and pried open the door. Two squad cars pulled up with paramedics following behind before he reached in to check for life. Officer Hudgens stepped out of their way. The other officers exchanged blank looks, waiting to hear Detwiler's status.

One of the medics yelled out, "He's alive. We won't know anything for sure, but it looks like he's been drugged."

Hudgens let go of the tightness in his lungs and breathed. He saw the others do the same.

The mood among the officers shifted. They looked at the house, their relief about their fellow officer replaced with the grim possibilities of what they might find. Officer Hudgens had been one of the officers present when Patti came out of the safe room. He expected a repeat of that incident. However likely, he could not take any chances. He drew his gun, motioned to the others to follow him or to cover the sides and back. He walked without sound to the front door. With everyone in place, he reached down and tried the knob. It turned and opened. He called out, "Patti, are you okay? We're officers checking on you." No answer.

He reached in to push open the door. Another officer joined him in giving a thorough room-by-room search. They found nothing on the first floor, second floor, or garage, so they took the stairs to the basement. The others had joined them now. Officer Hudgens experienced a rising irritation for the woman. They would find her again in that damn room, safe and unharmed, feeling no responsibility for not calling 911 when she knew she was in danger. Most of the men here had been with him when they found her, and he suspected they all had the same idea. They approached with caution until they were in front of the steel door.

Unlike the previous visit, the door stood open, the interior easily accessible. Officer Hudgens reached out to open the door further, keeping his body away from the opening. Because he was behind the door, he was not the first to see the scene inside, but when he saw the contorted expressions on the faces of the other men, he knew it would be bad.

Someone had battered the woman's face until all they saw of her face was tissue and bone. She looked like someone had peeled the skin off her face. He saw welts all over her arms and chest, swollen and puckered, and both palms scraped to the bone. He could not reconcile the victim in the scene with the woman who just days ago came out of this same room frightened and apologetic.

Monday Afternoon

Edgar waited at the airport arrivals curb, watching people pour out through the sliding glass doors looking for a taxi or shuttle. He glanced down at the photo on his phone to compare with women with Esme's general appearance. She came out, clutching a small bag and her purse. She appeared to have the same idea, looking down at her phone, and then scouring the crowd. He got out of his car, and waved her over.

"Hi, I'm Edgar. Glad to meet you." Esme resembled Elizabeth with that same casual air, but came in an edgier shell.

"Nice to meet you. I didn't think you really existed."

He did not know how to take that, but smiled. "I'm real."

Esme looked like she wanted to say something, but relaxed and said. "So how's Elizabeth?"

"She's shook up, of course."

Esme looked down at her hands in her lap. "I feel bad I didn't come sooner. I had to make sure things were covered at work since I don't know how long I need to stay."

Edgar sighed. "She refuses to go to the hospital. Maybe you can talk to her about that. This is the second time she's been hit in almost the same spot inside a week."

"Elizabeth has her own mind." She sounded so cryptic that he knew she meant to send him a message.

"I know that," he said. He opened the passenger door for her, and then slid into the driver's side. "Have you known Elizabeth long?"

"A very long time. I knew her when you two were seeing each other."

"I guess you disapprove of me?"

"I don't make judgments. Anyway, I don't know you well enough to have an opinion either way. Elizabeth draws her own conclusions about people in her life. I'm not her keeper. She doesn't need my approval."

Edgar thought she skated by that one easy enough and still had not answered his question. Better to leave that alone.

"So, what's all this ridiculousness about Walt's girlfriend," she said. "The whole scene sounds contrived."

Edgar wanted to comment that she was making a judgment, but checked himself. "I have to admit I'm curious from a spectator's perspective. I'm just glad *that* drama's behind us. I'm more concerned with who this nutcase is after Elizabeth."

"No ideas?"

"I haven't been around Elizabeth in years. I don't know anything about her friends or coworkers here. When she told me about the first incident, I thought it might be a spiteful teenager in the neighborhood. Or kids pulling a random prank. It's an immature attack, at any rate. But when she's attacked a second time, that changes things. She said she suspected Walt's girlfriend, Patti, our damsel in distress. Elizabeth saw a red paint can in her basement when we found her."

"I don't think I've ever known anyone who didn't like Elizabeth. Envious, maybe. For someone to feel so strongly against her enough to want to kill her doesn't click with me. Sounds like more fiction."

"Contrived?"

"Yes, now that you mention it," Esme said. "Elizabeth told me how Patti glared at her in the restaurant. Before that, she hadn't seen or heard of her. I'd bet money it would be her, if Elizabeth hadn't said she had an alibi each time."

"The first time, she was with Walt on their date. Wait a minute. The second time she was with Walt, too."

"Another coincidence? It seems all this started happening at the same time."

Edgar thought about that. "You're right. It might be time to take a look at all the circumstances as a whole instead of individual events."

When they arrived at Elizabeth's home, she looked pale and fatigued. "Esme, I'm so glad you came." Elizabeth got up and gave Esme a tight squeeze. "I needed a big bear hug."

"You look awful," Esme said. "Let's sit you down. I

thought Edgar exaggerated when he said he thought you see a doctor."

Elizabeth gave him a sharp look. "Thanks for filling her in. But really, I know it looks bad, but it's mainly bruising from falling that hurts so much. I'm surprised I missed the edge of the coffee table. That would've been nasty."

Edgar sat in a chair across from the two women, ready to get into a huff. With Walt and Patti out of their lives, he thought he had a clear road ahead of him. He visualized having her to himself, and finally catching up on the details of their lives the last six years. He had so much to tell her, so much to explain, and so much to admit. In some ways, he had been glad of Walt's annoying presence. It seemed to take the edge off his arrival. Now, this unplanned visit from Esme left little available opportunity to be alone with her.

Watching the two women talking, he remembered his attitude toward women when he was younger. He thought of them more as toys or amusements, interchangeable based on your taste preferences. It did not occur to him until recently that one woman could be so special that you would never forget her, even when you were lying next to someone else.

He noticed Elizabeth glancing over at him as she talked. She must have realized he had not spoken in several minutes.

"Sorry," Elizabeth said. "We didn't mean to shut you out of the conversation. We haven't seen each other in a long time."

"I understand. Why don't I take you both out for an early dinner? Afterward, I'll drop you back here and you two can visit."

"Thanks for understanding," Elizabeth said.

The truth was that he had a difficult time listening to women talk. Alone, he could direct the conversation, have a sense of being in control. Once they got together, the timbre of their voices, their irrational perspectives, and assertions of unsupported facts based purely on emotion tended to make him testy. His usual strategy was to make a discrete exit, easy to do around a woman you see every day. Not so easy when you had limited time to make your pitch. He committed himself to dinner, and she jumped at the opportunity. He wanted to size up Esme's influence on Elizabeth, anyway. Anything else had to wait until tomorrow.

They sat across from each other at a picnic table in a rustic restaurant at the edge of the desert waiting for their chili cheeseburgers, kettle fries, and beer. He wondered what Elizabeth was thinking right now while she and Esme had their heads together, deep in conversation about something worth gasping over every few minutes. All three looked up at their server with chunky arms carrying a serving tray.

"Enjoy," the stout blonde said and then turned her attention to the table across the patio. Edgar watched her moving away with a distasteful expression. He thought there must be a man somewhere who could feel love for someone he found so cheap and common.

"Well, this looks good," he said. "Do you eat here a lot?"

"Not really. I've only been here one other time. Old fashioned grub. Delicious, but very fattening. I don't think my arteries would last long if I ate here often," Elizabeth said.

All conversation stopped while she and Esme tore into their food. Edgar watched Elizabeth bite into the oversized burger, and cringed when ketchup oozed out of the side and ran down her hand. She caught it before it reached her sleeve.

"Excuse the hog, the pig knows better," she said.

"Gee," Esme said. "You can dress 'em up but you can't take 'em out."

Edgar watched Elizabeth laugh at Esme's rural analogy, which seemed to incite them to more goofiness.

"Wow, this is what I call fun food." Elizabeth said. She finished wiping off her hand down to her wrist, and tossed the napkin into a nearby trashcan.

Esme almost choked laughing with her mouth full of food.

"You almost need danger money to eat here," Edgar said. In spite of his usual disdain for poor table manners, he laughed with them.

"Elizabeth looks the part, doesn't she?" Esme said. "Banged up like she's been in a bar fight, swilling beer, and messing in her food. No wonder you picked this place."

Edgar did not indulge in fits of laughter as a rule, but he also fell into a hard laugh that tightened his stomach and forced out guttural grunts. The corporate world had no place for bad manners and jocularity. Meetings he attended were formal, stoic, and brief. Outside of that element, he found it easy to have a good time.

He could not be sure who laughed the hardest, but both women laughed until they cried. They had collected their senses when Elizabeth's cell phone rang from the depths of her purse. She glanced at its blinking screen, and looked up at Edgar. "It's Walt. Do you think I should answer it?"

"Go ahead. If you don't, I'm sure he'll expect a call back later. He's probably calling to thank you," Edgar said. "Put him on speaker so we can all talk."

"Hello."

"Elizabeth, I'm sorry to bother you again," Walt said. "But this time Patti's really dead. They found her this morning," His voice sounded strained, airless, as if he had the wind knocked out of him.

Elizabeth gasped. "What! I thought the police were keeping an eye on her place."

"An officer had been sitting in his car on the street in front of her house. Another cop found him drugged and unconscious."

"Walt, Edgar here with Elizabeth and Esme. Is the officer alright?"

"I don't know for sure, but he isn't dead. Just out of commission from what I've heard. I thought this was behind me, but they're looking at me again because I was the last person with her. I've told them all I know, but they don't seem to believe me. Can you call that attorney for me? I left the card you gave at home."

"My God," Elizabeth said. "Are you with the police now?"

"Yes, and I told them I'm not talking until I have a lawyer present. I don't think I'd trust a court-appointed attorney."

Elizabeth looked at Esme. "Walt, don't worry. I'll call him

right now."

Edgar sat back and watched the country-western band set up for their show while Elizabeth called her attorney friend. Esme seemed to be having her own private thoughts, but did not voice them. While he was sorry that Patti was dead, he could not muster up a lot of sympathy for her or for Walt. If he were honest, he did not like either of them. Just when he thought they were out of his hair, they kept popping back into his life like maniacal cuckoos. He watched the concern on Elizabeth's face as she detailed the situation to the person on the other side of the call. If he had to get involved again just to get this guy out of his life, he would do whatever it took. He gulped down the end of his beer and hailed the server for another.

When Elizabeth disconnected the call, she looked apologetically at both of them. "I'm sorry, guys. Bizarre, isn't it?"

"Do you think he did it?" Esme said. "Maybe he set up this whole scenario to get away with murder."

"I don't think so. He seems sincere enough," Elizabeth sipped her beer and made nervous glances at Edgar. "Ed, what do you think?"

"I don't think Walt has the intellect to orchestrate a plot this complex, but I'm not the right person to ask. I've only known them both a couple days. If I had to guess, I'd say little Patti liked to play games. If they hadn't found a body, I'd think she was behind a new elaborate hoax. But it's hard for me to say that for sure."

"At least he'll have an attorney to protect his rights. I can understand why the police think he's the most likely person to suspect."

Esme stopped munching on her fries, took a drink. "With him in jail, we'll be able to rule him out if your mysterious attacker strikes again."

Edgar perked up as if he had been in a dream state. "Damn. That never occurred to me."

Monday Night

Elizabeth could sympathize with Edgar's mood shift. She noticed the change in him during the drive back into town, but what did he expect? When you show up in someone's life unannounced, you cannot complain about what might be happening. Besides, she could not turn her back on Walt. He needed help. She did not believe the new theory that he might be her mystery attacker. This newly planted suspicion had gotten to her for a brief time until she realized he was Patti's alibi both times.

As for Edgar, he had always been serious, but now had taken on a sharper edge. Competitiveness and ambition had drained him of the casual approach to the world around him. Like most men she met, he took himself too seriously. He had lost the ability to laugh at life's practical jokes. She reached over and rested her hand on his forearm.

"I'm sorry," she said. "This hasn't been much fun for you since you've been here. I mean, you came here to sweep me off my feet, win back my love, and the happily ever after scenario.

"No need to ridicule me. I know how fantastic it sounds. You're right to want to help Walt. I'm being selfish. We'll have plenty of time to talk about what's ahead for us once we solve this new mystery."

"Good, I'm glad you understand," she said.

Esme sat in the back not saying anything. Elizabeth knew that meant she was saving up her comments for later when Edgar went home, but that's what friends were for, right?

Edgar interrupted her thoughts. "Listen, you remember the private investigator I called? He called back with information. Since Patti had already turned up, I didn't see any reason to mention it, but now it's worth considering."

Elizabeth saw the tension leave his face and a smile form. She and Esme leaned closer toward him to hear what he had learned.

"So, give us the scoop. Anything interesting?"

"Quite a lot in light of what's happened," he said. He gave them the facts Sam relayed to him. "Maybe we should ask Walt if he knows anything about her marriage. She might have mentioned hearing from her ex-husband when the threats started. I would think her ex would be the first person she'd suspect."

"What a story. You're right. When the police dig all this up, I bet they'll stop focusing on Walt."

"Let's get on the computer and see what we can find out about the ex-wife, too," Esme said. "There should've been articles in the paper at the time. It hasn't been so long ago that the archives would not be available."

Edgar grinned. "You two are having fun, aren't you?"

"I know it's terrible," Elizabeth said. "I'm sorry anyone should be murdered, but I barely laid eyes on her. Now, the idea of trying to solve a real crime appeals to me as long as the bad guys don't come after me. I mean, haven't you ever wondered if you could figure out a crime in real life? I've read mysteries since grade school. I can figure out a whodunit fairly well in a book because the clues are laid out for the reader. I've learned to spot the clues the author plants along the way. There're no extraneous facts, no irrelevant events. Everything has a meaning. In real life, that's not true. Anything can be related or have no connection at all. The detective has to figure out what has meaning. The unknown elements are what could make this a challenge."

"I wouldn't mention this to Walt," Edgar said. "He might get the wrong idea about you finding entertainment in his dilemma."

"You're right," Elizabeth said. "I guess I got carried away. I'd forgotten poor Walt."

"Let's decide what we need to learn," he said. He pulled into Elizabeth's driveway and put the car in park. "Sam gave me names, so we'll start there. Esme, are you good on the Internet?"

"I love it," she said.

"Good. I'll send Sam's notes over. What's your email

address?" He typed as she read off the letters. "Esme, if you can start searching, I'll call Sam when I get back to the hotel. I hope he'll have time to find the ex-wife."

"Good place to start," Elizabeth said. "What about me?"

"You need to rest. That's the least you can do if you're not going to get checked out."

She did not like to be bossed around, but passed on telling him so. Esme got out first. Elizabeth leaned over and kissed Edgar lightly on the lips. "Thank you for being understanding on all accounts." She opened the door and got out fast. He waited for them to get inside the house and turn on lights before he backed out and left.

Once they got inside, the two women fell into the sofa and exchanged looks.

"What d'you think?" Elizabeth said.

Esme coughed out a laugh. "He's charming, handsome. The authoritarian type. I get what you see in him."

"Yeah, but what do you think about him coming back?"

"I'm not sure. He believes what he says, but maybe there's an underlying dissatisfaction with his life. I'm reserving my opinion until we see what he does *after* this trip. Protect your heart first."

Elizabeth smiled. "You read my mind."

"I'm still hungry. What kind of snacks do you have? I need nibblies while I work on the computer."

"Have I got the thing for you."

Elizabeth made a large bowl of popcorn drizzled with real melted butter, poured sodas into large tumblers, and settled in next to Esme in front of her computer on a side chair from the living room. She leaned in to watch Esme's fingers travel quickly over the keys until she found a people search site. She checked Edgar's notes on her phone, and looked at Elizabeth.

"What town did they come from, did you find out?"

"Some small town in California that I'd never heard of before. I think it's Ojai."

"Are you sure? How do you spell that?"

"No idea. What about Southern California, then."

Esme typed in Abigail Bradley, her married name, and listed only California in the address field. The computer paused and blinked before bringing up a long list of choices. Knowing from previous experience that even separate listings could be of the same person, she ran the pointer over the most recent selection and waited for the payment screen to pop up. It was not free, but it was not that expensive. Elizabeth reached for her wallet and a credit card.

"Use this," she said.

The site went through its machinations until the *view report* button popped up. Esme pressed enter. She downloaded the file, and they started to read the report in front of them.

"There's not much here, is there? What a waste of money."

"It looks like Patti lived a clean life," Esme said. "Nothing to suggest trouble at all from what I can see here. I think hers is what the police refer to as "low risk lifestyle."

"I hoped we'd find something earth-shattering that we could take to the police," Elizabeth said. She could not disguise the disappointment in her voice.

"I'm just guessing here," Esme said. "But I would think the police could run this type of background check on her and probably already have. Since Patti's committed no crime, her name might not come up for a protection order, and as divorces go, protection orders might be commonplace. It might not occur to them to look beyond that trouble as anything other than a domestic dispute. What we need to do is point them toward the situation that ended her marriage, and the threats from the Cyril, and the stepdaughter's mother, Phyllis."

"I thought we could do more," Elizabeth said. "But you're right. Maybe the best I can do for him is pass this on to the police and his attorney."

She scrolled through the phone's address book and pressed to connect to the lawyer. She spoke when the voice mail prompted her. She gave him the police detective's name, and added Sam Shelton's name, and the past marriage and those details.

She also called the police department and asked for Detective Macy. She left a message on his voice mail, too.

"Hey, Elizabeth. Look at this." Esme pointed to the newest local headline on the homepage. "The young officer found outside Patti's house died from an airborne poisonous substance they haven't identified yet. I hope for Walt's sake he's innocent."

"You don't think they'd harm him in custody?"

"I didn't mean that. What I meant was there would not be leniency in their sentencing if he were found guilty of two murders, especially poisoning a cop."

"What a frickin' mess," Elizabeth said. "I just had a chill run down my spine. This situation is starting to scare me. It's a good thing for Walt that he didn't know Patti long enough to have a reason to hate her that much to go this far."

Tuesday Morning

Edgar did not choose to be brought into this situation, but since he had, he had to do more than sit around moping because Elizabeth was spending too much time with her friend. He needed action. His first task was to call Sam Shelton.

"Sam, Edgar Hamilton here."

"I didn't expect to hear from you so soon. What can I do for you?"

Edgar took a deep breath. "Same investigation. New developments. Patti Slocum, Abigail Bradley, whatever we call her, was murdered yesterday."

"Well," Sam said. "The first question should be which of her two identities was murdered."

"They're one and the same woman."

"Not really," Sam said. "Patti Slocum only existed in

Phoenix. If someone murdered Patti, that means you're looking for someone in Phoenix that met her during the time she lived there. On the other hand, Abigail Bradley has plenty of past. Whether she did anything to deserve it or not, we know of two people that might be viable suspects. We also have no idea how many others, such as Bradley's extended family, who might also harbor a grudge. The list of suspects for Abigail Bradley is incomplete and unknown."

"I hadn't thought about it like that, but you're right. I guess I should start with the ex-husband."

"I found his information before. I'll text it to you. What else would you like me to do?"

"I guess this is going to take looking into everyone's past, including Walt's. Elizabeth doesn't know much about him except what he's told her. There could be something pertinent."

"Got it. So Walt Perry, Cyril Bradley, his ex-wife, Phyllis Bradley, and both of their extended families. What about the murdered woman?"

"Sure. I met her mother, so I wouldn't be surprised to learn there's madness in the family. She could have a crazy cousin after her."

Sam laughed. "Stranger things have happened. I have time this afternoon to work on this. I'll get back to you tonight or tomorrow first thing."

"I appreciate it. Tomorrow then."

Edgar checked his text messages, wrote down Cyril Bradley's number and address, and made the call. He could tell as soon as the conversation began, the man did not want to talk to him.

"I'm tired of the whole situation," Cyril said.

"Listen, Cyril. The woman's dead. The police picked up a man she's been dating. He might be guilty, but he might not be. I'm only trying to get the bigger picture of her personality. You know, what kind of woman she was. Did she get along with everyone or was she antagonistic."

"Alright, but make this quick. My children are on their way

back from their grandparents' place."

"The first thing I want to know," Edgar said. "When was the last time you spoke to Patti, or Abigail? Did you know about her new name, by the way?"

"No, I didn't know she changed her name. Childish behavior if you ask me. The last time I saw her…" Cyril said. He paused now as if thinking about this with more dread than recollection. "I guess it was over three years ago. I remember she still had the old cell phone number because she told me that she was changing that number in addition to moving. The protection order was still in place, but was about to expire unless she went back to court. She said she was moving out of state to get away from the whole ugly situation—her words. She just wanted to tell me one last time what an asshole I was. I told her I would track her down like the dog she was and murder her in her sleep for the trouble she caused my family. She told me that my family was already troubled when she met me. There were other choice remarks by both of us, and then she hung up."

"So that was that?" Edgar said.

"After she'd been gone for a few months, I started to cool off. I guess as time passed, I gained a perspective and realized there was some truth to what she said. I guess I had found it easier to blame her than to take that hard look at myself. To be honest, if I had known where she was, I would have apologized to her. Everything between us went ugly so quickly. If anyone thinks raising children by shared parenting is easy, I'm here to tell them it's not."

Cyril paused. When he started talking again, Edgar thought he detected an emotional crack. "I was a fool, and I said horrible things to Abigail that I can never take back. I'm sorry she's dead, but I had nothing to do with her murder. I don't know who did."

"How about your ex-wife? What's her relationship with Abigail?"

"Very bitter."

"So, are you saying she could commit murder?"

"Anything is possible with that woman, but she's so self-centered, I can't see her doing that if it doesn't bring her under the spotlight. I haven't seen her for over a month. If you really think she could've been involved, you might want to track her through her family. She was never very close to them, but she kept in touch by phone regularly"

"Did she come from a big family?"

"Her parents divorced and remarried so there were half-siblings on both sides. She never really talked about the halves. As far as she was concerned, she never referred to them as her family, only her full-blooded sisters and brothers—two of each."

"Cyril, I appreciate you taking the time to talk with me. You've had a damn hard time, and I'm sorry to hear it. You sound like a decent guy."

"I appreciate the sentiment. So much loss. Once someone is gone, you lose all those opportunities to tell them how much they meant to you. I'm not making that mistake with my other kids."

Edgar resolved that he would not either. He said his last thank you and goodbye and hung up the phone. He sat back on the pillows on his bed. Talking to Cyril had exhausted him. He had to do something to distance himself from Cyril's sad life. He took a shower and invited Elizabeth and Esme to ask her to join him for lunch.

Tuesday Late Morning

Macy looked down at the information on the computer screen. With the information coming to light about Patti's marriage, the order of protection, and her flight to evade her ex-husband and the daughter's mother, Macy and his partner Stokes, considered any of them to be as likely suspects as Walt when you took in the short travel distance. More if you considered the daughter's death. With approval from their captain, they got an early start at four to make the tiresome drive to California. After checking in with the local police department there, who provided them with the data they had on the family, they drove to Cyril Bradley's house accompanied by a local officer.

The ranch-style house sat at the end of a cul-de-sac and looked like the owners were on vacation with its overgrown lawn and newspapers piled up by the door. Showing up unannounced did not always guarantee your suspect would be home, but they had learned from prior experience that there was little chance a guilty person would make a run for if he were confident he got away with his crime.

The man who answered the door in grey sweats and espadrilles looked fatigued and haggard. His dark blue eyes expressed confusion. When he spoke, his baritone voice sounded hampered by emotional undertones.

"Yes? Can I help you?"

"Mr. Bradley. Mr. Cyril Bradley?" Macy said.

"Yes. Can I help you?" he said again, sounding more authoritative than at first time.

"Mr. Bradley, my name is Detective Macy and this is Detective Stokes from Phoenix, Arizona. And this is one of your local police officers, Officer Samuels. We would like to have a few words with you about your ex-wife."

"Which one? I have two, you know," Cyril said. He did not try to hide his irritation now that he understood what they wanted.

"Abigail."

Letting out a large sigh, he said, "Sure, come on in," and opening the door wider, he turned his back on them to lead them to the living room. "That other man already called me to ask me about her. I'm emotionally drained. If I were a drinker, you'd have found me drunk just now."

"What man called you?" Detective Stokes said.

"Edgar Hamilton. He said he was doing a favor for a friend

trying to get background on Abigail. He wanted to know when was the last time I talked to her, then about our marriage. It's not so simple that you can tell it in a few sentences. I'm afraid I gave him the blow by blow as I saw it. I told him I'd gotten over blaming Abigail for what happened to my daughter, and I wouldn't have killed her even if I were still angry."

"So he told you she's been murdered?" Stokes said.

"Yes, I'm sorry about that. Abigail didn't deserve to be murdered. She had her peculiar side, but she was all right. If I'd been a better husband to her, things between us might have worked out," he said, lowering his head and closing his eyes. "Hell, if I'd been a better husband the first time, most things would have been different."

"Why don't you tell us what you told Mr. Hamilton? We need to know about her background as much as possible. Even things unrelated to your situation can be important."

Cyril let out a louder sigh this time. He looked up at the ceiling and then back to the officers while he repeated his story as he had done with Edgar,

Macy and his partner kept impassive expressions, a product of their years of experience in interrogating suspects. Cyril regarded them as he talked. Macy thought he expected to reveal something damaging about himself. Cyril paused to allow them to ask for clarification, but they remained silent until he finished.

"Well, that's about all I know. I realize now that my ex-wife fueled the fires and my feelings of guilt during a difficult time. I didn't manage my emotions as I should have. God, I asked myself later what I would have said to my children if they had that type of pain. I wouldn't have encouraged it, by any means. I guess having an angry, bitter ex-wife is just my curse."

"Have you spoken to your ex-wife recently?" Strokes said.

"The last time I spoke to Phyllis was about a week ago, before I went on this last business trip. I lied to Mr. Hamilton about that. She told me how she had found out Abigail was living in Phoenix and was going there to expose her to her new friends. Make her life a misery. I told her to leave it alone and worry about her other two children, but she just cussed me out and hung up. I haven't heard anything else from her. Do you think she's in Phoenix right now?"

"She could be, but she could be anywhere," Stokes said.

"She's travelled a lot since the divorce," Cyril said. "Usually with one of her boyfriends."

"Naturally, in cases like this, we ask this question to everyone involved. Can you provide an account of your movements in the last two weeks?"

"Sure, I went to Philadelphia to meet with a client. I'm an architect, you see, and I specialize in luxury home market. This client wanted me to be on site when I met with the surveyor, the geologist, and the general contractor. I got back last night. I can show you my plane tickets and hotel bills if you doubt me."

"For the record, I would appreciate that, sir, and your client's name," Detective Stokes said.

"Well, be discreet, for Christ' sake. This is an important job, and I don't want him to think I'm suspected of a murder." Cyril's expression showed visible alarm.

"That won't be a problem. I'll be discreet, sir. We're not out to destroy anyone, but we have to do our job."

"Alright then. I've had all the drama I can stand. I just want to take care of the rest of my family and work on my career."

While Stokes appeased Cyril and wrote down his Philadelphia client's information, Macy moved casually around the living room to position himself in front of the fireplace. He had noticed the photo gallery on the large wooden mantel, and someone in the photos had caught his eye. As he inspected each photo, some framed in pewter, some in wood, he saw an individual standing with several others in a group. Most likely, a family photo since they all resembled each other, but whose family, he thought.

"Excuse me, Mr. Bradley, I was just admiring your picture collection and could not figure out who these people are," he said pointing to an ornate pewter frame with wooden embellishments.

"Oh, they're Phyllis's family. Actually, her half brothers and sisters, her full-blooded brother and sisters are in that other photo. Her father married a second time and they had about five or six children. I haven't actually met any of them, but I keep those out for the children. My wife, I mean ex-wife, had a real love-hate thing going on with her half-siblings. She couldn't get over that her father left her mother, but she eventually thought of them as family."

"Nice family. On both sides, it looks like. So, you say she wasn't close to them. Do you know if they spoke regularly?"

"Thank you. As far as that goes, I'm not sure what her contact was before, during, or after our marriage. We had a lot of family, but didn't get together with either side much. We were so busy and all," Cyril said.

"We appreciate your help, Mr. Bradley. May we call on you again if we have any other questions?"

Cyril looked at both men with apprehension. "Certainly. Please take care when you call. I don't want my kids exposed to any of this if we can help it. They're still fragile from losing their sister."

"We understand. Thanks for your time. We'll do our best not to cause you any problems," Detective Stokes said. The three policemen walked outside. "I don't think he was involved. He has a pretty good alibi."

"You're probably right," Macy said. "But we still need to check on him."

"Sure, but I bet you'll never guess who I saw in that photo," Macy said.

"Who?" Stokes said.

"The man we suspected from the beginning. The man who said he hadn't known Patti very long. The man who is always 'Johnny on the Spot.' The half-brother I saw in the photo. Little Maggie's uncle, Walt."

Tuesday Afternoon

Elizabeth leaned forward in her booth at the Matrix while Edgar told her and Esme about his conversation with Cyril Bradley. She had ordered a big meal, but lost her appetite to the excitement of listening to him relate details and inserting his own personal observations of the man. For all the drama of the moment, she reflected on the strange turns in life. Here she sat with Edgar, absorbed in the lives of people they never met or had any reason to care about, as if all of this was a minor distraction they cooked up to amuse themselves. Esme played her part as the faithful sidekick, and that afternoon Patti Slocum's murder was the most important thing that any of them had on their minds.

When he got to the sad parts, she and Esme sipped their wine faster than normal to force down emotions. When he finished, they were quiet for several minutes taking in the ordinary sounds and smells of the restaurant.

"That's the saddest thing I ever heard. How horrible," Elizabeth said. She took a large gulp, and went back to moving her food around the plate with her fork.

"I can't believe he had anything to do with all of this," Esme said. "He has those other children to raise. No one could care as much for one child and regard his other children any less. Their mother, on the other hand, sounds like a slow-burning wick on a stick of dynamite."

"You're a curious girl, Elizabeth," Edgar said. "You have unexpected depths of emotion. Just when I think I have you figured out, I see another side to you."

She smiled. "I guess now we wait for Sam to call back with details on the families."

"Not if you two came up with anything," Edgar said.

"Oh, my God," Elizabeth said. She spoke so loudly, others in the restaurant turned their heads in her direction. "How could we be so collectively unfeeling? What about Patti's mother? She must know by now. I bet she's in a bad way. Why didn't we think of her?"

"You're right," Edgar said.

Esme looked from one to the other. "Didn't you say she has a screw loose?"

"Yes, but that wouldn't mean she would take her daughter's death without feeling. We should go over there and check on her."

"All of us?" Esme said. "Wouldn't it be better if I stayed here and watched our purses?"

"Yes, all of us," Edgar said. "Safety in numbers."

"You two are awful. I'm sure she's not violent. Only a touch delusional. Surely, she needs someone at a time like this. Tell you what, why don't we go over there before the dinner rush. We'll stay for a few minutes and then go."

Esme and Edgar exchanged looks, but Elizabeth ignored them. "Come on. This won't take long."

They piled into Edgar's rental. Elizabeth flashed on her teenage years when her gang of friends crammed themselves into the car belonging to their only friend who had one. She remembered the joy of having wheels, that new freedom when you were sixteen.

Edgar parked in front. They got out and stood looking at the house. "I bet she's in there crying her eyes out," Elizabeth said.

Edgar looked skeptical. Esme stood back a little ways behind Edgar. Elizabeth rolled her eyes. "Now, she might start on that stolen underwear story, but don't laugh. And whatever crazy thing she says, don't either of you look at me. I'd hate to burst out laughing when she's suffering from the loss of her daughter."

"We promise. Let's get this over with." Edgar had adopted Esme's same apprehensive expression.

"Honestly, you two." Elizabeth sniffed and led the way to the front door. She pressed the doorbell and stood back. They heard someone approach the door.

This time, Verna Kilgore opened the door right away. "What are you doing back here?"

"We wanted to see how you were holding up," Elizabeth said.

"Come on in," Verna said. She swung the door open and stood aside, watching them enter single file. "Are you here about my Abigail again?"

"Yes," Elizabeth said. "We wanted to say how sorry we are and to find out if there's anything we can do for you." Elizabeth noticed sheets covered the television, pictures, and the mirrors this time.

"Sorry? About what?"

Elizabeth froze. Had she been wrong that the police would have come here to notify her of Patti's death?" "Has anyone been here recently?"

"Yes, some cop came here earlier telling me some nonsense that my daughter is dead. I told him they need to hire better detectives if that's the best they've got. Abigail's not dead. I talked to her just an hour ago."

"Ah," Esme whispered. "She's in denial. Thinks her dead daughter's coming back." She paused for a few seconds, and then said, "Are you sure? The police seem positive."

"Oh, so they've told you the same thing. Like I said, they need better detectives. Now, if they really want to investigate something, they should look into all those crying babies I keep seeing in the mirrors. They're everywhere now. I finally had to cover mirrors to have some peace. The poor little buggers. Someone should do something to save them."

Piercing chills ran down Elizabeth's back. The woman really was insane.

Edgar moved toward the door, Esme inched in his direction. "We're sorry to have bothered you. We've been misinformed."

"It was nice of you to drop by."

"Elizabeth," Edgar said. "We'd better get going and leave Mrs. Kilgore in peace."

Elizabeth said, "Of course. I'm sorry if I upset you."

"Don't worry, dear. You meant well."

The three moved through the front door as quickly as they

could without running.

"I'm going to have nightmares tonight," Esme said. "Crying babies in mirrors. Oh, Lord."

"She's worse than she was before. Maybe Patti's death pushed her over the edge." Elizabeth knew her hands were trembling, but she could not feel them.

"Let's get out of here before she comes out and calls us back in," Edgar said. "We should've remembered the bad smell. I need to get cleaned up."

"Drop us at my place. I have to get ready for work anyway."

When he had dropped them off, Esme looked at Elizabeth. "What kind of people are you messing with here in Phoenix, Murderers, maniacs, and adulterers. Maybe you should rethink this move. Denver's safer."

Elizabeth thought for a moment. "There've been a lot of weird things happen since I got here, but I figure I'm under a karmic cloud. Once it passes, I'll be fine."

"If you live that long," Esme said. "I think you should be careful of her. Insanity's one thing, but there's even more than that going on with old Verna Kilgore."

Elizabeth sat at her desk in the Matrix back office lapping up the foam on her espresso while she made the work schedule for the coming week, placed food orders, and returned calls to suppliers. She had a meeting with the kitchen staff at four thirty, so she had the time to take a break and enjoy the coffee. The quick shower to de-skunk after Verna's house snapped her out of the malaise. Esme was right—as usual, she had allowed others to suck her into their chaotic lives. She was a mere bystander. She cared what happened to Walt, but beyond that, she had no emotional investment in Patti's wellbeing or the people in her life that kept her spinning her wheels like her gerbil did when she was a child.

Getting close to three in the afternoon, the restaurant had few patrons. Most of the staff was due back at four to prep for the later part of their split shift. She watched Antonio, who worked all day, tend to the straggling patrons in the main dining area. That was when she noticed the light streaming from the open door. The outside light coming from behind him hid the man's face in shadow. She headed back to her office, assuming Antonio would take care of the customer, but he stuck his head around the door to say Walt wanted to see her.

Elizabeth went out to the reception area to greet him. "Hey, Walt, we thought you were in jail."

"They can only keep you so long without charging you and my time was up. The lawyer you recommended might have had something to do with it. I don't feel like I'm out of the woods yet, but at least they can't find any evidence to prove I did anything wrong. This has been a nightmare."

"Have a seat," Elizabeth said. "Edgar and Esme should be here any minute. If you're hungry, I can get Antonio to put something together."

"I hadn't thought about eating. Now that you mention it, good food sure would help. My stomach's been in knots."

Elizabeth reached up to signal Antonio, and asked him to make up a dish of something for Edgar. The staff here all knew and liked Walt from when she date him and knew what menu items he liked.

"After eating those bologna sandwiches, I'll never be able to eat that again without remembering that cell."

Elizabeth smiled reflecting on Arizona's infamous sheriff known for his no-frills, no-nonsense philosophy that kept getting him reelected for so many years. She had always thought of the sheriff's public image as a great caricature of himself, and that he was someone with the right temperament for the job. But she was sure Walt's experience would leave him with a much different impression of the Phoenix law enforcement machine.

"I hope it wasn't too awful. I can't imagine what it would be like, and I hope I never find out," she said. Out of the corner of her eye, she saw the front door open again, and

Edgar and Esme come in. She waived them over.

"Walt, you've escaped?" Edgar reached out his hand to Walt's. Elizabeth frowned at Edgar's misplaced humor.

"Walt, this is Esme. I'm sure you remember me talking about her. She came to my rescue after the second whack on my head."

"What do you mean?"

"Sorry, you don't know," Elizabeth said. "Someone jumped me after Edgar dropped me off at home the other night. I'm okay. It looks worse than it is."

Walt's expression went gray. "I'm sorry to hear that. Did they catch the guy?"

"No," Edgar said. "I could've, but I stayed back to make sure Elizabeth was alright.

"When Esme heard, she flew right out," Elizabeth said, and took hold of Esme's hand. "I'm lucky to have a friend who cares for me the way this one does."

"Walt, I'm glad you're here," Edgar said. "Did Elizabeth tell you about the progress I made this morning in finding out about Patti's past. I spoke with her ex-husband."

"Oh, you mean Cyril," Walt said.

Elizabeth and Edgar looked at each other, and then looked back at Walt. "You knew about him? You're not holding out on us, are you?"

"Didn't you mention his name? Patti must've told me. So what did you find out?"

"He seems to have come to terms about Abigail's part in all of it. He said Phyllis, the ex-wife, is still out for her blood though. He said he hadn't talked to her in a month, so he doesn't know where she is. The good news is either one of them have a far better motive than the one you're supposed to have."

Walt looked down at his napkin on his lap. He avoided their eyes, and instead watched Antonio approaching with a serving tray over his left shoulder. Edgar, Esme, and Elizabeth stole looks between them, but said nothing while Antonio served Walt a fresh duck sandwich, pineapple coleslaw and thinly sliced fruits on the side. When he had gone, Walt looked up as if Edgar had just finished talking.

"That's good. Takes the focus off me. Maybe that's the reason they let me go."

"I only talked with him this morning, and I haven't had a chance to talk to the detective working on the case. They told me he was out, so I said I'd call back later."

"Well then, I guess now they'll believe I had nothing to do with this. I'm innocent, but if they don't believe me, I don't have any proof that I didn't do it. It sure feels good to have the two of you on my side. There's no telling where I would be right now without your support."

"We haven't done too much," Elizabeth said. "As a matter of fact, we haven't found out anything useful at all. I mean nothing that the police would not have found out anyway. By the way, what did the attorney advise you to do?"

"He sat in with me during questioning, and told me not to say anything unless he was present," Walt said. His face took on a worried expression, and his demeanor changed. "I didn't do this. I wanted to break it off, not kill her. I would have to be a real psycho to kill someone just because I thought she was controlling."

"You never said that before. What happened to make you think that?"

He turned his eyes away. "Listen," he said. "She had the kind of personality that she didn't treat people very well once she got to know them. I told you how I met her at the museum. Well, it was fun at the beginning going around to the museums, seeing plays, going to lectures. It's just that after a while, I got the feeling she was treating me like a project, like trying to transform the sow's ear. That's the reason I wanted to end it. That last date was miserable. She dragged me to a lecture at ASU, and kept hinting about taking classes. She wanted to control everything around her. I had a brief change of mind after we found her in the safe room, but then I started to have my doubts whether she staged the whole incident. I decided that if I were having those suspicions, I needed to back off again. Of course, right after I left, someone murdered her, but I didn't do it."

"I'm sorry," Elizabeth said.

Esme had been sitting back, taking in Walt's words. Esme looked like she had something on her mind, but Elizabeth thought it best to wait to draw her out later.

"Walt," Esme said. "I'm curious about what you said about her staging the incident. Do you think she was devious enough to concoct something that dramatic?"

"Of course," Walt said. "She had a sharp intellect, methodical, organized. If something required planning, she could do it. The question would be, why bother? The more I think about it, the more I know she wouldn't do that for me. I don't believe her feelings for me were that strong."

"What if she knew Phyllis came to Phoenix," Elizabeth said. "Either she hid as she explained, or she made up the threats to blame Phyllis as a way to get rid of her."

"That's possible," Edgar said. "There's real evidence of the stalking in California.

"Right," Elizabeth said. "So, what if she staged the scene like you said. That doesn't explain why she's the one found dead in her own safe room."

"No. That the fallacy in our theory," Esme said. "We're going to have to do better than that to get the cops to look at Phyllis."

Walt stood up. "Thanks for the sandwich. I'm going to get out of your way. Go home and have a shower. I can still smell the jail. I wanted to let you know I was out. I especially want to thank you both for the effort on my behalf. I appreciate it."

"We'll let you know if anything new occurs to us," Elizabeth stood and gave him a platonic hug. He gave her a weak response, nodded to the others and left.

When the door closed behind Walt, they looked at each other. Esme raised her eyebrows. Edgar kept a fixed stare at the door. Elizabeth watched them until she had to speak.

"The whole thing is too contrived, isn't it? I feel like I'm in the middle of a B-movie."

"Something is sure fishy," Esme said. "I get a sense Walt is not telling us everything."

Elizabeth gasped. "You're right. He's careful. He doesn't speak with the ease you'd expect."

"I wonder if there's another reason the cops suspect him," Edgar said." One that doesn't sound as lame as the one we're hearing about."

"I wonder too," Elizabeth said.

Tuesday Evening

Macy drove all the way back to Phoenix. Stokes had driven there and now fought to keep his eyes open. Maybe the decision to do a turnaround was not the smartest idea. Six hours both ways with four hours in between crammed full of activity and interviews. He pulled into the parking garage at the Central Station. Neither had eaten, and both needed a rest, but Macy knew he and Stokes would be back on case as soon as they reached their desks. First, they needed to check in with the boss to give him the update.

"You two look rode hard and put away wet," the commander said.

"It was all worth it," Macy said. "Briefly, we found out that Walt's half-sister is Cyril Bradley's first wife, Phyllis. She's the mother of the girl that died while in custody a few years ago. She holds Abigail to blame. I mean our Patti Slocum. She told Cyril she found out Abigail moved here and headed her to get her revenge."

"You don't say. I remember that case. Made national news. Pretty young girl dies while in police custody. The press couldn't get enough of showing the wretched parents vowing to sue someone as soon as they figured out the who."

"That's the one. We figure it like this," Stokes said,

"whether Walt came here before, and happened to run into her, or came to Phoenix specifically to find her, he had to be in on it with his sister. Patti probably didn't know who he was and fell right into their plans."

"Do we have any physical evidence to support your theory?"

"Not yet. We'll bring him back up for another interrogation. Put the facts in front of him. See if he cracks."

"That's going to be difficult. His lawyer got him released this afternoon. You'd better have something solid before you bring him in again. He could claim this was a big coincidence, police harassment, and all that crap."

Macy looked at Stokes. He knew they both were cussing inside about the lousy timing.

"Yes, sir. We'll work that angle. They always make a mistake somewhere." Macy nudged Stokes's arm to leave.

"Damn," Stokes said.

"This changes the scope of this investigation. We know Walt and his sister are in this. All we have is a pile of circumstances, but now that we're on the right track, we'll find the evidence. It's only a matter of time now."

Wednesday Morning

When Walt got the call the next morning from Detective Macy, who had said he had more questions for him, he had not placed too much significance on it. After all the questioning before, he assumed they wanted to go over more of the same. Keep repeated the questions to try to wear him down or catch inconsistencies in his answers that might reveal some important clue. He thought he was getting better at the interview process, like getting used to ill-fitting shoes. He chuckled as he walked into the main lobby and asked the man behind the glass barrier for Detective Macy. Even when Detective Macy came to the front to meet him and he was buzzed into the inner sanctum of the detectives squad, he had no idea that he would be confronted with anything he had not heard before.

They led him to another interview room and he sat down at the conference table where he observed his image in the mirror across from him. He expected someone on the other side. Most likely, there would be a camera running or someone would switch it on once the interview started. Relaxed and confident, he tapped his fingers on the table and contemplated his cuticles.

It had been a half hour before Detective Macy returned to the room and seated himself at the opposite side of the table. Each man looked into the other's eyes. The air in the room was close, and a faint but lingering smell of disinfectant brought to mind scenes of vulgarity requiring a thorough removal of the unpleasant stench of voided body fluids. In the first few seconds after Detective Macy sat down, the room filled with the smell of anxious anticipation. Walt somehow realized this meeting would be different from the previous encounters. They continued to stare each other down until Walt's eyes started to burn. He blinked and averted his eyes.

"Is your attorney late?"

"No, I didn't call him. Why keep paying him to sit with me while you keep asking me the same questions over and over."

Macy read Walt his rights. When he finished, he said, "I have to ask you formally if you are waiving your right to an attorney during this interview."

"Sure, why not. Unless you're actually going to arrest me this time." Walt detected a change in attitude from before, and regretted not calling the lawyer.

Detective Macy took his time speaking. He looked stared directly into Walt's eyes.

"We've come across new information that requires an explanation on your part. Do you want to tell me again about your relationship with Patti Slocum, or should I say Abigail

Bradley?"

"I told you before. I met her a couple of months ago at the Phoenix Art Museum. We had a relationship, but nothing serious, at least from my point of view. I had decided not to see her again on that last date. When she went missing, I was concerned like anyone would be if that happened to someone they knew. When we found her, I was glad to help. She was so upset and didn't seem to have anyone else."

"So you're saying that you didn't know her before you came to Phoenix?"

Walt felt his nerves starting to falter, but he had to keep it together. "It sounds like you're implying something. Just come out with it?"

"Alright," Macy said. "Why don't you tell us why you concealed the fact that Patti, aka Abigail, was married to your ex-brother-in-law?"

Walt closed his eyes to take stock of his position. This was bad. He knew how it looked. No story he made up now would sound as ridiculous as the truth. He decided to take his chances and tell him the events as they happened.

"Listen, I told the truth when I said I met Patti here in Phoenix a couple of months ago. Sure, I know about Abigail Bradley. My whole family knows, but we never met her. If you know anything about my family, you'll find out that the children from my dad's first marriage resent us from his second marriage. Each family group goes their own way. My dad grieved over the fact that Phyllis and her siblings turned out as bitter as their mother. As kids, we never formed a bond with them, got close, you know. We learned to accept it. As we've all grown older, some of them, like Phyllis, started trying to establish a relationship.

A few years ago, she started to call me occasionally. I figured out she couldn't get anyone else to listen to her. When Cyril remarried, I think she went a little nuts. I knew she had abandoned her kids, so I didn't have much sympathy, to be honest. Her whining went in one ear, out the other. It sounds hard to believe, but I never laid eyes on Phyllis until she got here."

"So when did you hear from her last?" Macy said.

"I talked to a couple of weeks ago. She said she found out that Abigail had moved to Phoenix. She planned to find her and make her miserable. She never once said anything about killing her, though. I thought she had a lot of anger and used her ranting to ease her own guilt. If I thought she could be dangerous, I would've done something about it."

"When you talked with her, she didn't say she knew Abigail had a different name?"

"No. If she knew, she would've gloated over learning a fact like that."

"She didn't contact you when she got here? I'd think she'd want someone on her side."

"Well, yes," Walt said. "We met for dinner the night she got in town. She jabbered on like before. One minute, she'd be so angry, the other folks around us would stare. The next minute, she'd cry. I felt sorry for her. I told her to call me before she did anything crazy. She promised, but said no one could stop her from what she had to do. And before you ask, all the time I knew Patti, she never told me about her name change or any of the problems with an ex-husband. In fact, she told me next to nothing about her past. She was too occupied with working on improving my mind."

"So you're saying that when Patti went missing," Macy said. "Or when we thought she went missing, you had no idea of her true identity or who might have been responsible for the threats."

"I swear. Not until the day after I took her home from the hospital," Walt said, starting to sweat. "Of course, I recognized the name in the county records. I thought Patti rented the house from Abigail, and only pretended to own it to impress people. I still had no idea they were the same person, even when Elizabeth said the mother claimed she only had a daughter named Abigail. That morning, when Patti told me the whole story, looking for sympathy and asking me if I thought any less of her, I panicked. The truth came over me all of a sudden, and it shook me up, I can tell you. Realizing what a horrible coincidence I stumbled into, and dreading Phyllis's reaction when she found out. She'd believe I tried to protect Patti. Patti would believe the same thing as you—that dating her was part of a plot. I couldn't get out of that house fast enough. Then when she turned up murdered hours later, I couldn't think what to do. I thought if I said nothing, no one would find out."

Macy leaned in close. "But those kinds of truths always rise to the surface during a criminal investigation. Why didn't you come clean with this information when we interviewed you before?"

"I couldn't be positive Phyllis had anything to do with it. I wanted to talk with her first, even if it seemed likely she found Patti's address and mailed those letters. I decided I didn't want to implicate her until she admitted what she'd done, but I haven't been able to reach her. As I said before, my sister is a real coward. She has no problem screaming and threatening, but that's only when she's sure the person won't fight back. I can't believe she would actually kill anyone."

"We'll be the judge of that. Give me the numbers you have for her," Macy said. He slid a pad of writing paper in front of him.

Walt wrote down the Phyllis's home and cell numbers, and slid the pad back to Macy.

"I'd also like to check your cell phone activity. Any problem with that?"

"No. I've told you everything I know." Walt pulled his cell from his shirt pocket and handed it to Macy.

"That's what you said before." Macy carried the phone out with him, leaving Walt alone in the room.

Behind the mirror, Stokes had been taking notes when Macy joined him. Both men looked at Walt, who was not looking as confident as he had when he first arrived.

"What do you think?" Macy said.

"He's believable, but that doesn't mean it's the truth."

"I have to agree. We suspected his involvement from the

beginning, but for a different reason. This gives us a stronger case. Family loyalty can be a strong motive. He's trying to play like they weren't close enough for him to want to avenge her, but I'm not buying it. I bet he knows where she is and what happened. He has the strength necessary to do that extent of damage on Patti's body—only a man or a very strong woman could do that. But we see those types of attacks by men more often than by women. And, he has sufficient know-how to disable a security system, too."

"We need to get all the information we can on Phyllis Bradley. Let's also find out what we can about the rest of the brothers and sisters, too. She could be an isolated nutcase, or she could be a part of a family of crazies."

"Good idea. In the meantime, what's your opinion of him?" Macy said, pointing his thumb at the window.

Stokes frowned in concentration, his eyes staring and focused.

"He looks like he's telling the truth, but I don't want to let him loose yet. Let's keep him here for further questioning, at least until we can get confirmation on his story."

Later, as Walt sat in the small cell and tried not to inhale the acidic odor from the urinal, he had many thoughts chasing each other across his mind. Anger at not having the sense to bring his attorney to the interview. Regret that he moved to Phoenix in the first place. Disbelief his sister could kill, much less kill in such a brutal manner. Everything felt wrong. From the first few actions and everything subsequent to that, he had an uneasy feeling that everything was not as it seemed. The very idea that he would meet a woman whose background tied closely to his started to sound unbelievable to him, too. He could not blame the police—he would suspect anyone in his lame position.

Then he had to think about Phyllis. He had no idea where she was right now. Her last call was days before Patti said the threats started. That was suspicious, he knew. She came to

Phoenix on a mission to threaten and intimidate Patti. Then, with all of her pent up rage, she took her misery and guilt out on the person she blamed for everything bad in her life during a savage confrontation. That sounded plausible if you did not know Phyllis. He learned from all their conversations that she found it easy to attack with words, but she had never physically assaulted anyone. As far as he knew. Maybe she went over the edge, and turned into a different person.

He had time to think it through while he sat there. Somewhere in all this, he would find an answer. Focusing on the past events in their logical sequence gave him the best opportunity to connect what he had seen, but had not attached any significance to at the time. He had to consider possibilities that he would have thought ludicrous before.

Even thinking about Elizabeth and Edgar, he found himself getting suspicious of their motivation for helping him. Granted, he had asked her to get involved, but who knew anybody in this town. People moving anonymously in and out of a city so large and impersonal, missing neighbors went undiscovered, and new acquaintances' backgrounds never questioned. He only had their word for whom and what they were. Maybe he was getting paranoid, but he was sure someone had not told him the truth, and he had to figure out who before the police had so much evidence against him, he could not get out.

Wednesday Early Afternoon

Elizabeth sat next to Edgar at the Matrix listening to Macy tell them about Walt's connection to Patti's past. Both of them sat spellbound with dropped jaws. Esme returned from the bathroom. She looked about to speak, when Elizabeth put her finger up to shush her. Esme sat down, and looked up at Macy.

"He swears he didn't know who Patti was until she told him her story the day after the rescue," Macy said. "He said he'd been shocked and caught off guard. She expected him to be sympathetic, but he said he had acted badly and ran out on her. He swore he'd never visited Cyril and Phyllis while they were married and had no reason to be friends with Cyril once he remarried. It's true that he hadn't left Corinth when Maggie died. Their families aren't close enough for that. He had only seen the obituary notice"

"So he knew who she was after that records search and didn't tell us?" Elizabeth pressed her lips together. "I feel so gullible. I guess you were right all along, Edgar,"

Macy ignored the commentary. "We were right that he had not told us the whole truth. For the present, we believe we have a strong case for accessory, if not for the actual murder, we're still investigating all leads."

Elizabeth stared ahead in anticipation of Macy's next comment. She had scooted close to Edgar when Macy first came in. Now their sides touched, his hand held hers. Elizabeth was more upset than angry. Finding out Walt deceived her upset her more than she would have expected. Esme and Edgar witnessing all this made the betrayal more humiliating. She knew what they would be thinking now.

"Mr. Hamilton, Edgar, I wanted to ask you about your contact with Cyril Bradley. We interviewed him the same day you called him. He told us about the details he gave you about his family. Is there a particular reason you did that? More importantly, if you do not know any of these people, why get involved in all this?"

Edgar cleared his throat. "The private investigator told me she had changed her name and why. He told me her real name, that she had been married, and how she had filed protection orders against Cyril and Phyllis Bradley for threatening her. I didn't know the details, but I decided to call the ex-husband to ask him about her."

He tightened his hold on Elizabeth's hand. "As for why I'm involved, Walt asked Elizabeth for help because he was afraid the police suspected him in Patti's disappearance, and he did not know many people here. Since I'm here, I offered to help as Elizabeth's friend. I know how to get to the bottom of things. Besides, I wanted to get rid of him, and I thought the best way to do that would be to help clear him."

"I can understand what you're saying, but I'm curious," Macy said, "why you took it upon yourself to interview this man. Do you realize you could have jeopardized this investigation by your actions? What if he's involved and you've alerted him to what we know. Not to mention your personal exposure, if he had been a viable suspect."

Elizabeth saw Edgar glare at him, red-faced and self-conscious in front of her, taking time to regroup before speaking. Elizabeth kept her expression frozen and tentative. This reminded her of two bulls going head to head fighting for dominance. She wanted to laugh, but thought neither man would appreciate her humor at this moment.

Edgar cleared his throat. "I don't think the dramatics are quite called for, Detective. For one thing, you were only concentrating on Walt—not on Patti's history. When I found out about the protection orders, I knew I had to get more information before I went to the police. For another thing, I made a telephone call, which is not the same thing as dropping in on a stranger. I did not and do not feel I put either of us in jeopardy by making that telephone call. I will also remind you that you had not said you suspected anyone else other than Walt, so it's not as if I stepped on police's toes. Even now with all you've found out, you obviously still do not suspect her ex-husband."

"That's not the point, and you know it. I'd appreciate it if in the future you have any information that might assist us in solving this crime that you call me directly instead of trying to play detective yourself. Is there anything else that your private investigator found out?"

Edgar gave him a chilling look of disbelief and said, "No."

Detective Macy stood up and scooted the chair back under the table. "I'll be seeing you," he said, and left the restaurant.

"What a jerk," Esme said once the door closed behind Macy.

Elizabeth saw Edgar still fuming from the official reprimand. He needed a change of perspective. She looked at Esme and winked. She turned to face him. "Well, what do you make of Walt now? After everything we tried to do to help him and he lies to us like that. It would've been a lot simpler for him to tell us about the connection rather than pretending to be in the dark all along. Letting you waste time and money on that private investigator. It makes me wonder if I ever knew him at all. I'm so sorry that I got you involved with the whole thing."

"Now, wait a minute," Edgar said. "You didn't drag me into the situation. I wanted to help you help him, and I'm glad I was here. I've been suspicious of Walt's motives from the start. What if he committed murder, and you helped him on your own? You could have ended up the same way Patti did. No."

"I don't know Walt, either," Esme said, "But I've always thought he knew more than he let on."

"I wouldn't want another ass-chewing like the one I just got again, so let's do this the right way," Edgar said.

"Macy sure does reprimands well," Elizabeth said, resting her hand on his leg.

"I'll get over it. I guess I'm not used to dealing with cops, or having my judgment questioned. He could've been right about the danger. I hadn't considered that. All I have to say about Walt right now is that I hope for his sake that the cops find another suspect. If they don't, I don't believe he'll get out of this." Edgar looked over to Elizabeth who suddenly had a pained look in her eyes.

"I suppose," she said, "that we've done all we can do?"

"What else can we do? We don't have the resources the police have to track down a missing person in the form of Phyllis Bradley. If we knew where she was, we could call Macy, he would pick her up, and they might be able to get to the bottom of this. As it stands, Cyril said he doesn't know where she is. He thinks she might be on vacation with one of her boyfriends, none of whom he knows or has ever met."

"I guess we can visit Walt in jail and see if he will tell us anything," Elizabeth said.

Esme choked. Edgar flinched.

"You want to talk to him after we just found out he lied to us?" Esme looked more startled than before.

"Wait," Elizabeth said, putting her forefinger to Edgar's lips, "before you two say anything else, hear me out. I'm not saying he was right to lie, but what if he lied because he knew we'd assume he was guilty? It's possible, you know. What if he really had nothing to do with this, but is charged and convicted anyway? What if there's something we could do to help, and we don't? What if he's executed, and later we find out we could've done something to save him. They have the death penalty in Arizona, you know."

Edgar rolled his eyes. Esme went quiet. Elizabeth kept her face impassive, and continued, "What if one of you were in his spot? Wouldn't you want someone on your side?"

"You really want to go to jail, I mean, visit him in the jail," Edgar said, "and ask him about his sister?"

"I don't see anyone else we could ask. Her family members might not want to talk with us as frankly as Cyril did with you. Walt should know her habits and maybe places she would stay, or even the family members she might contact if she needed a place to hide. He would know what she had to say about Patti the last time she called him."

"I don't think this is a good idea," Esme said. "Didn't you hear what the detective said five minutes ago?"

Elizabeth ignored her, more because she knew Esme had a good point.

"I think we should make a list of what we want to ask him so we don't forget. We should ask him if he thinks she's capable of such a horrific crime, in the first place. If he says no, that would be a start. Then we can ask him exactly what she talked about during their last conversation. Would there be someone close enough to her that might help her hide. How technical was she?"

Edgar said, "What's that got to do with anything?"

"Well, if she's technologically challenged," Elizabeth said. "We could question whether she'd be sophisticated enough to learn how to disarm the security system in Patti's house. And to know how to get into a safe room."

"Good point," Edgar said. "Of course, you remember that Walt admitted he knew a lot about safe rooms."

"I know that, but we're working on whether his sister had the ability."

"Okay. What else?"

"Let me think a minute. What about if she called anyone else the way she did him, you know to complain about Patti. Did she mention anyone else who hated Patti as much as she did? Do you think we should be writing this down?"

"I don't think they'll let us take anything in with us. They might, but why take the chance? We'll use our superior memory retention instead," Edgar winked. "Let's leave it for now. By the time we get into see him, questions will come automatically from his responses to our questions."

"Sounds good," Elizabeth said. "We can walk there from here, but we should hurry. I have no idea what visiting hours are."

"Listen, you two. I can't go to jail. Cops frighten me. I can't even stand to walk past a police car without getting hives. I'll wait here. But I still say this is a mistake."

Edgar erupted in a raucous laugh that made them jump.

"What's so funny," Elizabeth said.

"You talk like we're going to visit a sick friend in the hospital, and Esme makes it sound like we're marching up the steps to the guillotine."

"Stop it," Elizabeth said. "Call this number to verify his location and the hours we can go." She handed him her phone, pointing to a number for with the Fourth Avenue Jail on her browser. "I'll check on the staff in the kitchen and be right back."

When she returned, Esme pulled away from Edgar.

Elizabeth knew they were talking about her bad judgment. Even if they meant well, she couldn't help being annoyed.

"Visiting hours end at five," Edgar said. "That should give us fifteen minutes to get there and a two-hour window to get in and see him."

Esme stood up and hugged Elizabeth. "Be careful in there. I mean it. Don't walk off by yourself. Anything could happen."

"I'll be fine. Stay here, have something to eat, and relax. Nothing's going to happen."

Elizabeth took a last look at Esme as they walked out. Poor Esme.

"What are you grinning about?"

"I need to explain. She saw an old movie about a woman who visited someone in an insane asylum, and got trapped when she was mistaken for a patient. Esme's never gotten over that. She thinks that can happen. She included jails and prisons into her paranoia, too"

"Interesting. But she's not all wrong. About getting involved, I mean."

"I'm a grownup. I can accept the consequences of my actions, if necessary. Don't worry about me."

They set off walking down the middle of downtown Phoenix on First Avenue toward the jail.

"Edgar, you've gone quiet," Elizabeth said.

"Walking in this sun like this, I'm missing the moist air and cooler temperatures back home."

Elizabeth wondered if his thoughts ran more to the irony of coming to Phoenix to find the woman, but finding himself involved in a murder investigation instead.

Wednesday Late Afternoon

Elizabeth and Edgar sat across from Walt in the public

meeting room. He looked tired and beaten. In the last few days, Elizabeth noted his coloring had lost its Midwestern pallor that contributed to his wholesome looks, but instead of a deeper suntanned tone common to Phoenicians, his complexion had gone gray and dingy. Phoenix was not agreeing with him. If there was ever an end to this mess, she knew he would not stay.

A sudden wave of sadness came over her that surprised her. She had been the one to break it off with him, she reminded herself. She remembered how suffocating his presence had been, the constant calling, or texting, the uninitiated visits to her house. He was too needy and dependent. The relationship would never have worked, so why the sense of loss? Edgar's voice brought her back to task, forcing her to address her feelings later.

"How are you holding up?" Edgar said.

"I guess as well as can be expected," Walt said. "I guess by now you know my family history and that I knew of Patti before she changed her name. I swear I did not always know who she was. I didn't find out until after we found her, and she told me her story. When I realized who she was, I couldn't believe it. How could I tell the police I suddenly knew her? I'm surprised you're here, knowing that I concealed the facts."

"I won't lie. I have reservations about you and your story," Edgar said.

"Edgar!"

"I'm sorry, Elizabeth, but that's how I feel. Having said that, Walt, I'm willing to keep an open mind. If I weren't, I wouldn't be here."

"I appreciate your honesty," Walt said. He looked at Elizabeth. "He's being honest. It's fine. Really."

"Before we get down to what we wanted to ask you, why don't you tell us everything you know. When you talked to Phyllis, what she said, any plans she had made, that kind of thing," Edgar said. His voice was not as tight, but almost tolerant. Walt had that effect on people.

They listened while Walt told them his story. It matched

what Macy said he told him earlier. When he finished, he shook his head. "Phyllis had a plan to come here to frighten Abigail. To make her life a misery, as she described it, but not to kill her."

"Would she have told you if that was her plan?" Elizabeth said.

"At the time, I wondered. I warned her not to do anything rash. I worried she'd show up at Abigail's door and attack her. I told her she could end up in jail, especially in her irrational state. And then, she got in touch when she first arrived in Phoenix."

Elizabeth stared at him. She wondered if he admitted this to the Macy.

"We met, had dinner—the only in-person meeting we'd ever had our entire lives. She was furious and grief-stricken, a real mess. She had not found Abigail's address yet. Then she admitted the only reason she contacted me was to talk me into helping her. Neither of us knew about the name change, so looking for her in the telephone directory didn't help."

"What about the public records, like how we looked up her house?"

"I hadn't thought of that, but then again, I wasn't motivated either. I'd gotten tired of listening to her. The way she seemed to me, if she weren't in a rage about Abigail, there would've been some other target. That's the type of person she is."

So," Edgar said, "as far as you know, she never found her. Now, in the light of what's happened, don't you believe that Phyllis not only found Abigail, but beat her to a pulp as well?"

"I don't know what to think anymore. No, I can't believe it deep down. Crazy or not, she had no history of violence. Ask anyone in the family."

"Did you try to call her when all of this started?" Elizabeth said.

"I tried calling many times, but her phone keeps going to voice mail."

"Who else does she consider a confidant?" Elizabeth said.

"She must have someone else she would've called to help her. What about her brothers and sisters, for instance?"

"Her mother was very bitter about her dad's remarriage. I'm sure that's where Phyllis got her anger. Most of the children on her side of family are mean and hateful. They don't like outsiders, but sometimes, I don't think they care for each other any better. Remember, Phyllis moved away from them. I finally figured out that's why she called me. I'm the only one who answered her calls."

Edgar took a deep breath. "So, all we know is that she arrived in Phoenix and met with you when she couldn't find Abigail. Assuming you're not involved, Phyllis had to have found Abigail's address by herself, and then went there for her final showdown."

"I know it sounds like it had to be me or Phyllis, or the both of us are working together. I know I didn't do it. I can see how, you not knowing Phyllis, you'd wouldn't know that threats are more her style. To cause someone to fear a mysterious unknown enemy would give her satisfaction. The threatening notes—that I can believe."

"Do you think she might have lost control seeing Abigail in person after all that time?" Elizabeth said. "You know, like she was her normal self until the object of her rage was in front of her, and she went into a blind fury?"

Edgar regarded Elizabeth, and said, "Good question. You always hear that everyone has a breaking point. An emotionally charged situation instigating an unstable situation. What do you think, Walt?"

"I hadn't thought of it in those terms, but it's possible. She is a high-strung female."

"I almost forgot to ask," Elizabeth said. "Did she have the technical skills to work out the security system? And do you know if she had any knowledge of safe rooms?"

"I only know what she would say in the course of our conversations over the years. She couldn't even set her sprinkler system. If she had a power outage, she'd call her handyman to reset it. Of course, when she was married, Cyril did all that type of thing. She had brains, especially if she studied something with a manual to learn tasks, like adjusting the thermostat or the intercom system. I know it doesn't make my case any stronger, but I don't think she could do this. I'm a better candidate."

Concentrating hard, Elizabeth said, "Could we be looking at this all wrong? Maybe this has nothing to do with Patti's past life as Abigail. Maybe this is about someone none of us knows about. For instance, Patti could've dated someone before you knew her, but after she arrived here in Phoenix. Say that person held a grudge about something."

"Interesting alternative theory," Edgar said. "What about it, Walt? Could there be someone she dated before you that she might have mentioned? Even if she didn't mention a problem, there could have been hard feelings that she would not want to talk about."

Walt looked more hopeful. "I wish I did know something like that."

"Well, give it some thought. Maybe even an event more than a person. Now, is there one of her siblings that might talk to us—one that would be likely to know where she is?"

"One of them might," Walt said. "Angie would be the most helpful. When you call her, tell her you're concerned about her sister. Don't mention me. And whatever you do, don't mention Abigail. Maggie's death is still a sensitive spot. None of the family would be sympathetic to anyone connected to that situation." He gave them Angie's last name and said he knew her house phone was not restricted.

"We'd better get going," Edgar said, taking advantage of a lull in the conversation.

"I'm sorry I lied to you both," Walt said. "I want you to know I appreciate you staying on my side. With any luck at all, I'll get out of here as soon as the police learn what really happened, and I'll do what I can to show my appreciation."

"Don't worry about that," Elizabeth said. "Just keep your spirits up. One way or another, I know this is going to work out."

Elizabeth took in a full breath of fresh air once they stepped out outside the building. She had to blink hard to force back her emotions.

"This reminds me of visiting my dying father in the hospital," she said.

"Why do you say that?" Edgar said, taking her arm during their walk back.

"Trying to say all the right things, assuring him that the situation is not as bad as it looks, that there must be something the doctors can do. Going so far as making future plans that you know can't happen for him. Even while I said all those things, we understood the subtext of the conversation—that I was trying to find a way to make the end appear not so inevitable."

"So you think he Walt did it."

"No, but I don't see how we or anyone else can prove it."

Thursday Morning

Early the next morning, Detective Macy barely sat down at his desk in the detectives' squad room before the telephone on his desk rang. The yellow blinking light informed him it was a call coming from within the network of offices that included both downtown jails, the coroner's office, and the forensic lab. After savoring a sip of the coffee he bought on his way in, he grabbed the receiver. "Detective Macy."

"Detective, I'm so glad you're in. I need to meet with you about a serious matter regarding a case. Do you have the time?"

Detective Macy recognized the voice of the unidentified caller because they had talked so often over the years. He knew Arthur Beddoes's voice instantly. The head of the forensic lab was a quiet man, and a man of integrity and honesty. Any time he felt it necessary to leave his lab, he had a strong reason, and the reasons were not always good for Macy's cases.

"I just got in and haven't had a chance to get started on anything yet, so this is the perfect time."

"Good," Beddoes said in a rushed and frustrated voice. "Be right up."

Detective Macy did not have much time to anticipate. Within minutes of hanging up, he saw the elevator doors open and the diminutive man in a white lab coat headed in his direction. Under his protective clothing, he wore an immaculately tailored shirt and slacks, sensible loafers, while his gray and balding head reflected the light from the harsh glow of the fluorescent office light. Not imposing, but he had the reputation of being the best forensic scientist in the southwestern United States. Phoenix PD knew they were lucky to have him. As he approached his desk, Beddoe's small gray eyes looked up into Macy's with an apologetic expression.

"What's up, Arthur. You look like a man with something on his mind."

"I had to tell you in person before you hear about it through the normal channels. There's been a mistake in the lab concerning the DNA results in your murder case. It's unacceptable that a mistake like this could be made on my watch by one of my people, but what's done is done, and we just have to make it right." The small man's face glistened with sweat.

"Good God, what are you talking about?" Macy said.

"You know we took samples of all the blood we found at the Slocum scene. There was so much blood all over that room that we went on the premise that some of the blood might have belonged to the killer. We took hair samples from the victim's hairbrush for elimination purposes. We took samples from the areas closest to the body, assuming they would test as a positive match for the victim, and took other samples farther away as possible residual splatter, or transfer from the killer."

"I got that," Macy said.

"When your suspect provided a DNA sample, we expected

we'd find a match to some of the blood we speculated would be the killer's. It wouldn't need to be much more than a finger pricked, you understand. The problem is that a lab assistant misidentified the sample. No one realized we had a problem until the results came back from the direct tissue samples from the victim. We identified the DNA from the hair sample from a brush belonging to the victim and compared it against the blood on the floor. The lab tech assumed we had a match and didn't follow through with a comparison. That's where we made a mistake, because when we compared DNA from the victim's tissue against all samples taken from the room, and then compared to your suspect's DNA to the same, we found a family relationship—a female relative."

Macy staggered back enough that other's around him noticed. "I'm stunned. This is the last thing I expected in this case."

"We were already faced with a dilemma because of the absence of dental records. By the brutal force used by the killer in destroying the victim's teeth and face. I personally took charge of the comparisons last night. All of the blood at the scene matched the victim—no one else."

"This changes everything," Macy said. "This means that in order for Walt to be a viable suspect, he would have had to have a motive to kill one of his female relatives. I think I can guess speculate with ninety-five percent certainty that the victim is Phyllis Bradley."

"Who?"

"Our suspect's half-sister. I'll call her ex-husband, Cyril, to find something to use for a definite match, but I'm sure. No scientific proof yet, just the police officer's hunch. This is going to mean releasing Walt. The case against him was largely circumstantial at best, so this leaves us starting over from scratch."

"I'm very sorry this happened. I can assure you something like this won't happen again," Arthur said.

"Mistakes happen. I'm more disappointed at myself. The brutality in the destruction of the face of the victim should have made me suspicious right away. I let the previous events lead me to a conclusion instead of looking at the scene for what it had to tell us. But that's what someone wanted us to do. And I think I know who that person is."

"As soon as I get those samples, we'll make it a priority."

"I appreciate you coming up here to tell me yourself. You're a good man," Macy said. The scientist extended his hand, they shook on it, and he hurried back to his lab.

"Damn," Macy said.

Stokes arrived in time to hear him. He sat at his desk in the next cubicle, and said, "What's that all about?"

"I just got some bad news. It turns out the victim is not our damsel in distress, but is probably Phyllis Bradley, the woman we've been looking for. We need to get something of hers to compare her DNA. Maybe the ex-husband can help us with that. We need to get Walt up here and ask him a brand new set of questions."

Thursday Late Morning

Without a positive DNA match, Macy and Stokes needed to be sure they had the right female relative before proceeding. Macy pulled the files on the case, while Stokes called down to the cells to have Walt brought up to the interview room. Walt was still the most important person in the case, not as a suspect now, but as a person with valuable inside information. If he could not help, they would lose more time investigating this murder that was already days out and in danger of growing cold.

Macy and Stokes stood up to acknowledge his entrance when Walt arrived. Macy directed him to the chair opposite them on the other side of the table. Walt eased into his chair, arranged himself although his clothing was loose, and looked from one to the other.

"New evidence has come to us that put a different light on this situation. We're going to tell you straight out that we no longer believe Patti is the victim. Our forensics lab has produced DNA results which reveal the victim is related to you." Macy paused to allow the news to sink in. When Walt did not speak, he said. "Walt, did you understand what I just said?"

"I understand what you're saying," he said, but he kept his eyes fixed on the table.

"You don't sound surprised. Why is that?"

"I don't know what you want me to say. All I can think is that you've put me through this hell for nothing."

"We're sorry about that. We were following the evidence that led to you as a suspect. It looks like Patti might be responsible for sending us in your direction."

"What do you want from me now?"

"We need to identify the body. Since we know it's a female related to you, we need to narrow it down. Considering her past connection with Patti, we think we know who it is, but we need a way to test her DNA for the match. Do you have anything of Phyllis's that she might have worn or used?"

"Not that I can think of. She never visited me and I didn't visit her. You might call Cyril to see if he has anything left over of hers from when she lived there. I know she said she had a couple of items there for when she picked up the kids, like hair brush, comb, toothbrush, that kind of thing."

Macy gave Stokes a look, and while Stokes left the room, he continued. "We can't announce a definite identification, but I think you'll agree with me the most likely victim is Phyllis Bradley. We need to track her movements from the last time anyone spoke to her. That's most likely you. We need to place her with Patti around the time of death either at Patti's home or elsewhere. We'll be checking on Patti's movements. And taking a much closer look at her life here in Phoenix. She never talked about her family or her background?"

"No. She talked about herself in a superficial way. I realize that now. She talked about what she knew about the arts, and her intellectual interests. We rarely talked about anything else. To tell the truth, I started not bothering to listen. She talked about being on her own. I assumed her relatives were dead except for her mother in London. Now, I know that's London, Kentucky. I told you how we found her living here."

"Now, during your talks, did Patti ever mention wanting to disappear? Did she mention a place she might want to move?"

"No, I thought she liked it here a lot. She never complained like a lot of us do who are new to the city. I had the impression she jumped right into the cultural society here."

"If you would, I want you to write down as much about her as you can remember. What she liked to do, favorite places, or anything that might lead us to a place she might go."

"I'll do what I can, but I don't know how little I know can help."

"You never know what small fact that might seem inconsequential might turn out to be important."

"I assume I'm free to go," Walt said.

"Yes. I'll get you out of here as quickly as possible." Macy felt the shift in the dynamics of the interview. There was more tolerance in his voice than before and less accusatory tone. While he sympathized with the man, he had to keep in mind that there was a wild chance that he was in on this with Patti. Unlikely from what they knew, but not impossible.

Walt wrote slowly and deliberately. He made a list of things he knew about Patti and handed it to Detective Macy, who told the waiting officer waiting outside the door to take Walt back and get him ready to be released. Macy watched Walt walking down the hall, more erect than before but still with the air of someone beaten by life. Macy continued to watch him until they were in the elevator.

When he turned around, he found Stokes standing there and realized he too had been watching Walt.

"Do you think he's involved?"

"It's hard to say," Macy said. "Probably not, is my gut feeling, but you never know. Walt has incredible self-control, but I don't think he's hiding anything else. If he hadn't lied about knowing Abigail Bradley, he wouldn't have looked so suspicious in the first place. He has himself to blame for some of this. He's guiltier of being a fool than a criminal."

"Patti Slocum or Abigail Bradley, on the other hand, is a different story. The drama, the theatrics, all of the panic. All an act. Just like Walt said, something didn't seem right when she came out of that safe room. She most likely worked alone. Her scheme had to be precise. You can't always count on a partner to be as meticulous in execution."

"I think we need to take a closer look at those threatening letters she *said* she received. I bet she knew who sent them and decided to use them to her advantage."

"Or she wrote them herself to set the stage. What I don't get is why."

Stokes looked thoughtful for a few seconds and said, "Well, she changed her name once already when she moved here. What if her reasoning had nothing to do with being afraid? What if she had a reason to keep moving and keep changing her identity? We can get our profiler to help us with pinning down her type. I'm going to do a background check on her. And her mother. We had taken Verna Kilgore for her word that her daughter's background was what she said it was."

"You have a good point there. Walt and Cyril would rely on what she told them. Most people don't challenge someone's background or make them prove it. Most of us take people at face value."

"Unless you're in law enforcement," Stokes said, showing a grin for the first time that day. They both laughed off the moment's tension.

Macy thought how lucky that they had taken Patti's fingerprints after the episode in the safe room for elimination purposes. They ran her prints against every database available, but came up with nothing. At least she was not in the system, local, national, or international, but that could be good or bad, they agreed.

"Let's find out if Abigail Slocum is her real name maiden

name," Macy said.

Phony documents were so commonplace, and criminals came up with new strategies almost as soon as law enforcement figured out the existing ones. Suspicions confirmed—no baby Slocum born on the date she listed on her driver's license in London, Kentucky, or anywhere.

"We need to pay a visit to her mother. Edgar and Elizabeth said she's crazy but surely she'll know her daughter's real name and date of birth." Stokes said.

"We'll see. Nothing surprises me anymore."

"We thought we had this case wrapped up. Nice and straightforward, but now it's looking like this one might go unsolved," Stokes said.

"I'm picturing her, hiding in a shadow or behind a door, waiting for the opportunity to pound the life out of her victim," Macy said. "Not just setting the stage to play dead so she could start a new life, but doing so to set up someone specific to take the blame and get rid of another enemy. She's cool, emotionally detached, and methodical. The idea doesn't set well that she's gotten away with this so far and is still running loose on an unsuspecting public."

"The worst part is she has a good chance of getting away if we don't find her soon."

Thursday Afternoon

Once he walked through the door of his home, Walt went straight to the shower, shaved, and changed clothes. He made a heavy meal of fried potatoes, scrambled eggs, and beef hash—his favorite childhood meal. The food brought back happy memories of his folks and the peace of their family home. Depositing a large pot of coffee on the kitchen table beside him, he lost himself in the piled up *Arizona Republic* newspapers from his front step.

The memories of the last week moved further back in his mind as unreal scenes that he had watched in a movie. He looked around the room. He took in the old-fashioned gas stove, and the other outdated appliances that he preferred. He studied each to remember later. He had come to understand that life in Phoenix was temporary. If nothing else could be sure, he knew he did not belong in Phoenix, but back in Corinth where he knew all of his neighbors, had generations of family, and had roots in the community.

He had stalled long enough. He closed his eyes to remember the tall trees and luscious countryside back home to keep from giving in to his nerves. He volunteered to call Cyril for an object belonging to Phyllis to send to the police here. Then the chore he dreaded the most—calling Phyllis's siblings. His own siblings would not care much, but his father, now old and fragile, peacefully sailing into old age with the love of his wife and their children, who fortified him against life losses he could not control.

Phyllis's death would be especially difficult on his dad since she never reconciled with him, excluding him from her life as punishment for leaving her mother. Now, he and Phyllis would never have the reconciliation he had hoped for. Walt wished he could spare him, but that would be crueler than truth.

He finished reading the newspapers, and then turned his interest to the bourbon that would help him get through the telephone calls. He sipped slowly, took a minute to savor the flavor, and to enjoy the warm, burning sensation as it trickled down. He took a deep breath and called the last number he had for Cyril. When he heard Cyril's voice, he almost hung up.

"Cyril, this is Walt Perry. Phyllis's half-brother."

"Walt, I guess I shouldn't be surprised to hear from you. It's my week for surprises. I've had the police and a man named Edgar asking all kinds of questions. If you're looking for Phyllis, I haven't seen her."

"Cyril, I don't know how to say this other than to say it. Phyllis is probably dead." He told him what he knew so far and then waited.

"Oh, my God." Cyril's voice rose to a high, hysterical pitch. "I knew she was a speeding car heading for a brick wall, but I never imagined this. And the police think Abigail did this?"

"It's starting to look like it. Listen, Cyril, I have to tell you that I dated her for a couple of months, but I did not know who she was. She was going by a different name, and I had no way of making a connection."

"Did she know who you were?"

Walt felt suddenly confused and disoriented. His perspective shifted to an uncomfortable place. "I have no idea. I was shook up when I found out who she was. I never thought about her knowing me. I thought it was an awkward situation, but only a coincidence. You think she might've set me up?"

"If you're telling me that she set up all of this, she's smarter than either of us gave her credit for. Maybe she wanted the police to accuse you of her murder; another way to punish our family."

"I'll pass this on to the detectives handling the case. It might make a difference. Speaking of which, they need something they can use to identify the body to be sure it's Phyllis. Is there a brush or comb or clothing around that you could send for them to use?"

"Sure. There's a whole drawer of hairbrushes, a curling iron, make-up, all sorts of things. I'll send them out right away."

"Good," Walt said. He gave Cyril the address for the Phoenix Police Department. "I've got to call Mom and Dad to tell them about this. I'm dreading calling the others though."

"Let me do it. It'll be better coming from me. They should take out their grief out on me. After all, I'm the one who married Abigail. They'll be angry, but not so harsh as if I'm from your side of the family. Are these detectives the ones they should call if they have questions? And you know they will."

"I assume so. Listen, Cyril, I appreciate the way you're taking this."

"I'm upset, don't get me wrong. We started out so much in love, with a bright future in front of us. Even after the marriage went sour, I still held on to the memories of the good times. There've been times I forgot what she turned into and only saw the beautiful young girl I married. I'm sorry she won't have the opportunity to find her way back. I lost her a long time ago, so I've already done my grieving."

"I understand you. At least you have those good memories to tell the kids. This is going to be hard on them, isn't it?"

"I'm sorry to say that I think it'll be easier for them if she's dead. She hurt them. Knowing she was around but never bothering to make time to see them. At least now, they won't have expectations that they might see her. It'll be over, and I can replace their disappointments of her with how she was before. Hopefully, they won't suffer too much in the long run from the damage she caused."

"You have to wonder what happened, but I guess it doesn't matter anymore now."

Both men were quiet, but it was a comfortable silence, a moment to honor the past before moving forward. Cyril was the first to speak.

"Call me if you need anything else. I'll get this stuff over to the police right away. Don't be a stranger, Walt."

Walt poured another inch of whiskey and tried to pull out from that dark place so he could call his Dad. Maggie's death, his first granddaughter, had sent the dear old man into deep depression. Now, he had to be the one to call with news of a murder in the family. Walt wished he could be there in person to give his father the emotional comfort he had generously provided his children. It would be up to his mother to take care of his dad until everyone could get over there. Walt closed his eyes, took a big gulp of his whiskey, swallowing without tasting and made the call.

Friday Morning

Macy could not sleep. He looked at his clock. Four in the morning. Something kept nagging at him about this Slocum case, but the piece of information eluded him. He ran the sequence of the case through his mind. He thought about Cyril Bradley and their visit to his home. Then he remembered what he had forgotten. That photo on the mantel. Cyril said they kept it out for the children so they had a connection to that side of the family. Patti had the opportunity to view that photo anytime over the course of their marriage. She would have recognized Walt as soon as she met him. He could be telling the truth from his own perspective, but he had not considered that she intended to run into him.

They arrived at their desks just before six carrying strong designer coffee loaded with double espresso shots and extra sugar.

"I saw Walt in that photo and never thought to think about the reverse situation," Macy said. "Patti knew who he was the minute she laid eyes on him."

"We thought he had murdered her. At the time, we had no way of knowing."

"Now that we know she's alive," Macy said. "Let's look more into her mother. That must be where she's been all this time."

"We have the address on Race Street. Let's take a ride over there."

"Did you check on her Kentucky address? If her mother still has a place there, we can contact the local department to stop by to see if she's there."

Stokes flipped on his computer screen, and started typing in the information he had on Verna Kilgore, and any known addresses in London, Kentucky. The search came up fast.

"Here's another fact we overlooked. Verna Kilgore lives in the London Care Facility," Stokes said. "She had a previous address in the same town until two years ago." He continued typing. "I did a reverse search for the address Walt and Elizabeth gave us. This doesn't belong to anyone in the case. Who the hell is Sandy DiCarlo?"

Macy started thinking. Stokes stared at him for a response, but he had to think about this."

"You look like you got something. Don't keep it a secret."

"Maybe we just found Abigail aka Patti's new identity."

"You think she'd drag her mother out of a care facility to help her with a scam like this one?"

Macy felt a laugh coming, he could not hold back.

"What is it? I hate when you do this."

"I'm starting to wonder if her mother has ever been here. What a way to hide. Pose as your own mother."

"Damn," Stokes said. "Now I think along those lines, you've got to hand it to Patti. Many women look like their mothers. With the right make-up and clothes, someone could age themselves to look a couple decades older. They sure do that in reverse easy enough."

Macy jingled his keys in his pocket. "Let's get over there. We're probably already too late."

They were lucky to get the search warrant so fast. Macy figured this situation was so overt, no judge had to take long to scrutinize the issues before making a decision. Macy chuckled to himself, but Stokes heard him.

"What's so funny?"

"Picturing us kicking in the front door of this house like they do on television."

Stokes laughed out loud. "Sure would be easier if police work was like it is on the screen. We'd solve all our cases."

"I'd like to solve this one."

The place looked quiet when Macy and Stokes pulled up in the driveway at Verna Kilgore's house. Stokes went to the back. Macy went to the front door. When he estimated Stokes had time to get in position, Macy knocked. No answer. He knocked again, this time moving over to the window to peek inside. He thought of their earlier talks about kicking in doors, and tried the knob. It turned and the door sprang open.

"Mrs. Verna Kilgore. This is the police. We have a warrant." No response.

He pulled out his pistol, and walked inside. The overwhelming stench caught him off guard, but he kept moving forward, keeping alert for anyone behind a door or in a corner who could jump him. So far, the place looked empty. The small kitchen, overrun with dirty dishes and rotting trash, had the least opportunity for someone to hide. He opened the refrigerator. Nothing more than minor food staples—eggs, bread, and the like. Then he heard a sound from the back.

He swung around, checked his surroundings again, and then started toward the sound. He made his way down the hall, and checked both bedrooms and the bathroom with no luck. He reached the laundry room that had a windowed door to the backyard. He peered outside, but saw nothing. Not even Stokes who should have been there. Macy's hair stood on end, his pulse started to pound. Something happened. He knew it.

Macy poised his gun, unlocked the door, and swung it open. At his feet, on the stoop, Stokes looked like a broken toy soldier, bent in an awkward position with what could have been fake blood running down the side of his head, except he knew it was real thing. He looked from side to side before kneeling next to his partner to check his pulse. Thank God. He called for backup and an ambulance.

He had time to think while he waited the short time before help arrived. They were on the right track. He knew that now. All they had to do now was to find a killer who was not only sly, but had no hesitation about killing again.

Friday Evening

By the time the setting sun made its descent, the sky appeared with hot pink with streaks of blue and yellow. Elizabeth had put out the fires normal to the restaurant business. From calling in a replacement for a no-show waiter, to rushing out to buy supplies missed in the daily deliveries, she had kept her focus on the frenzy she anticipated at the beginning of a busy evening. She had switched her mind to concentrate on work, leaving her thoughts about Walt and Edgar far behind to deal with later. The patrons packed the dining room all evening, and the staff worked like demons until the last customer left. No complaints, no tantrums, no temperamental outbursts from the kitchen. All good.

When she finally had time to slow down, she sat in her office with a comforting Bailey's and coffee. Stretching out on the leather loveseat, with her feet hanging over its arm, she carefully brought the tall glass mug to her lips. She would savor the memory of this ritual once she had moved on to another stage of her life. The din of the supper crowd filtered in but only as soothing background noise.

She took another sip, and meditated on the new developments of the murder case. It had seemed to her all along there was too much drama, too many histrionics. A real sense of theatre. But she had kept that opinion to herself. Having the tendency to voice her opinions too freely in the past, she had taken on a new approach—be quiet and let others figure things out on their own.

But her basic instinct had been right. Walt's half-sister was the one with her face bashed in. If it were not for DNA testing, this deception would have gone unnoticed. When she asked Walt about how mechanically inclined his sister was and he had said she was not, she remembered the inkling she had that something seemed wrong. The person with the best knowledge of that security system and the workings of the safe room was the owner of property herself. With the benefit of hindsight, the plot seemed so obvious now.

What was bizarre was how Patti thought she could disappear and get away with murder in this modern age of DNA profiling, interstate, and international criminal databases, fingerprinting, and even a monitoring system for US passport use. How anyone could get away with that, she thought. Of course, there would have been planning involved. Creating and developing a new identity probably took a good deal of time.

Elizabeth thought about that and imagined herself in Patti's shoes. Her first name changed happened through the court, but this time, she had to learn the criminal's way. Patti might start with searches on the Internet for names, locations to move to, and a new set of wheels. She wondered. She doubted the police had overlooked Patti's computer, but she might be lucky to find it still there. After what happened today, they would be sure to take possession of it. If she could get into Patti's house and her computer tonight, and if Patti had not wiped out the history, she might be able to find a clue about her plans by tracking her logic via the Internet activity. It was worth a try.

It had occurred to her that she might not have a lot of time once she got inside Patti's house. Best to know what to look for ahead of time. She sat up, went to her chair in front of her desk, and switched on her laptop. While she waited for it to boot up, she thought of ways to search for tips on changing your identity. If she had an idea of what was out there, she would know what to look for in Patti's web history.

After allowing the distractions of the latest gossip news, she typed in "how to change your identity." The search results found hundreds of websites and blogs, but Elizabeth went to the first one at the top of the list, figuring Patti might have done the same thing.

As she read the suggestions and instructions about how to establish a new identity with authentic documents, she guessed that Patti would have started down this path long ago. Legally changing her name was one of the ideas proposed. Throughout all the steps involved, from obtaining a fake birth certificate and Social Security card to getting new credit accounts, one warning was mentioned repeatedly: Have absolutely no contact with anyone or anything from your past, especially if you were changing your identity to escape a threat, such as a violent stalker or organized crime. Some of the information did not apply to Patti's situation, but so much did. She printed out pages for later reference, finished her Bailey's, and shut down her computer.

Elizabeth decided Edgar and Esme did not have the need to know. They would try to stop her. Both expected her to be working anyway. Esme had taken the rail to go shopping at Biltmore Fashion Park, and Edgar said he had business calls to make at his hotel. Elizabeth left the Matrix by the back door out to the parking space reserved for her car. She often left her car there instead of driving it home. While she had been warned of car thieves, she believed the car was safer there than at home. With security cameras and regular police passing by, she had not worried someone would steal her car, although she was not so naïve as to leave the keys in the ignition. Those, she kept in her desk drawer in case one of the employees had to move her car in a hurry for a delivery. She slid in behind the steering wheel of her Honda Civic, took a deep breath, and gave thought about how she would commit her first burglary.

Patti's bungalow was located on an older street with an alley running behind the homes. Although the city had not paved the alleys, garbage trucks and utility vehicles used them regularly. Some homeowners used the alley to access a garage built at the back of the property. Driving down the next street over, Elizabeth strained to see if the yellow tape was still up around the back door. When it was obvious that she would not be able to see from her vantage point, she decided to drive down the alley to look.

She took her time, creeping along to keep down the dust and avoid rocky debris that built up around some back fences until she reached the back of Patti's house. The tape was gone.

Surveying her surroundings, she weighed her chances of being caught. Most neighbors were watching television or in bed. Directly across alley from Patti's property, the neighbor had a well-kept back fence and a small-bricked driveway that led into a one-car garage. The garage and tall wooden fence gave her a place to park the car and keep it partially shielded from the streets on either side of the alley. She pulled the car carefully into the spot and shut off the engine. She listened for sounds of opening doors, scarcely breathing as she braced herself for someone to run up and tell her she was trespassing. She thanked the stars no one came.

She slid out of the car, pushed the door closed until she heard the lock engage, and slipped the keys into her pants pocket. She looked both ways one more time, and then walked through the chain link gate to Patti's back yard, keeping on the stone pavers that led to the house. Now that she was here, she realized she had not thought about a key. To her relief, when she tried the door, it opened easily. She rushed inside and looked behind her. If she were seen, it would look suspicious, so she said another short prayer, and kept going. Once inside the large kitchen, she closed the door and looked around.

Patti's house was not unlike Walt's in its floor plan with its eat-in kitchen, except this remodeled kitchen had black granite counters, cherry cabinets, and stainless steel appliances. Elizabeth found herself growing critical of yet another quote-unquote designer kitchen, and mentally commenting on the lack of imagination in homeowners that they would want to have the same exact kitchen as their neighbors.

She moved to the dining room, then to the living room, until she saw that Patti had turned her third bedroom into an open den by knocking out a wall to create an archway. The computer sat on the desk in the center of the room. She congratulated herself on getting this far. The full moon brightened the rooms enough to get around, so she had no need to stumble through the house. She could not take the chance on flashlights that flickered against the windows and set off alarms to the neighbors. She remembered the disposable plastic gloves from the restaurant kitchen. She flexed her fingers, stretched them over her hands, and walked to the computer. Another thought came to her that there might be items relating to Patti's new identity in the desk drawers or file cabinet. She turned on the computer so it would boot then opened the top drawer.

Everything was neat and organized, pens, mechanical pencils, stapler, and other miscellaneous office items. She looked inside the three drawers on the right side of the kneehole—only blank stationary, envelopes, copy paper, and postal supplies. The unlocked filing cabinet offered nothing. She turned her attention to the computer. The browser history showed Patti had not been online since last week. The sites she visited then were for travel clubs, weather conditions, climate readings, and native foods for South American countries, one in particular was Venezuela. Patti's email account opened without a password. Elizabeth found itinerary confirmations for a trip to Montreal and another to Vancouver.

Finally, information she could use. She had watched a program on identity theft. One technique used to disappear involved flying into Canada under your existing identity, then return with a new name under a new passport. The intention was to convince anyone that you had ran off to Canada. That must be what Patti did or was going to do. Elizabeth thought it was sloppy of her to leave the computer, but she might have been flustered after killing someone. She forwarded several of the recent confirmations to her own account, and then logged off, hoping that the police would not notice activity after the murder. She had second thoughts about leaving her own online identity, so she deleted the sent emails in Outlook Express and in the files buried deep in the core of the computer that most people did not know about. No doubt, that was not good enough to scrub her activity to hide from a computer forensic expert, but she might get away with it.

Mission accomplished. She should feel exhilarated, but became frightened instead, as if someone's eyes were on her. She did not believe in ghosts. Even if she did, Patti's ghost would be the only spirit she would be afraid of and she was still alive. She shrugged off her apprehension, and made her way out of the house the way she came. She looked around. The neighborhood looked uninhabited as she rushed out through the gate. She scrambled to get to her car, locked herself inside, and started the engine. She drove down the alley at a slow pace, until she turned onto the main street.

Elizabeth guided the car into its parking space behind the restaurant, hurried inside to her office, and locked the door behind her. Her heart was pounding. She reached into her portable refrigerator for an opened bottle of Pinot Grigio, pulled the cork, and drained the remainder into a glass. She leaned back in her chair, wine at her lips, and turned on her computer. She took a big gulp, and said, "Congratulations on your first covert operation, and praying no one saw me do it."

Friday Night

Elizabeth read Patti's emails one by one, scanning for anything that would reveal her new identity or location. She found responses from Venezuelan hotels and from airlines offering pricing and availability, but no reservation confirmations. She assumed that if Patti planned to go there, she would make arrangements under a new name. Elizabeth felt certain she had solved the puzzle of where Patti meant to go, but she kept reading each email, even the junk mail. She thought one of the junk mails might be important. An offer from an insurance company that could save her money on her new Mercury MKZ.

Patti drove a Toyota. Elizabeth's pulse started to throb in her ears. Could she be so lucky to have found this? She knew that many companies sold their customer lists for an additional revenue stream, and she knew that advertisements like these would make reference to something you actually owned to personalize the offers. What did not make sense is why use the same email address if she planned to change her identity. Could Patti be that arrogant?

After printing out the entire email message that included the sender's name, she noticed that Patti's email address was *1goingforbroke*. The thought occurred to her that Patti might do what so many others do and create new email addresses close enough to the original to make it easy to remember. We are creatures of habit and tend to carry certain habits and idiosyncrasies with us, even in disguise. From what she had read about changing an identity, the experts rated that as risky. Elizabeth hoped Patti made that mistake. She made a note of her idea on the printed email with several variations, like *goingforbroke*, *goingforbroke1*, and even *goinforbroke*, and then started listing the names with higher numbers. This list might help the police track her.

Thinking she had done all she could do, she kept reading and sorting through the other emails. The second to the last email looked like an anonymous advertisement, but on closer inspection, Patti had subscribed to the company's newsletter. The company, which sold raw land all over the West and in some eastern states, had sent her specific sales information based on her criteria. Without a password, Elizabeth could not get in to view Patti's preferences, but the knowledge that she had been looking for raw land was a big lead in her opinion. Again, she printed out the email and set it with the others.

Drinking wine the past hour had made her light-headed and vaguely silly. She had to eat something quick. After calling the kitchen to have someone bring her a plate, her cell phone rang. It was Edgar. She giggled. This is bad. He will know I've been up to something.

"Hello there," she said. "What are you up to?"

"I've been on the phone most of the day taking care of issues that came up at the office, and checking on things at home." She heard a stiff tone in his voice when he mentioned home. "What've you been doing all day without me? Not getting into trouble, I hope."

"Well…" she said, hesitating.

"What have you been up to, girl?"

"Well, I had this idea, see, about the case. Wait. Are you coming over? I'd rather tell you in person."

"That's one of the reasons I called. I wondered if you would enjoy a change in scenery, to eat somewhere different. But I have no problem eating there either. It's up to you."

"If you don't mind, I'd rather you came here. I already ordered my dinner. I can have a plate brought up for you, too. We can eat in my office so we can talk in private."

"Okay, I'll come right over. I had a light lunch anyway. Give me about fifteen minutes. Since you are ordering, I'll take the salmon dish."

"Good choice," she said breathlessly. "I'm excited to show you what I have found out."

Just as she hung up, someone knocked on her office door. She got up to turn the deadbolt, and said, "Enter," Expecting the waiter, she started clearing her desk. When the door opened, her heart sank as she looked into the accusing eyes of Detective Macy.

Busted like a child caught in the act of doing something sneaky. She forced a smile and asked him to sit down. Aware that he was looking at the stack of printouts on the corner of her desk, she put her laptop in sleep mode and smiled.

"What brings you here, Detective?"

"Oh, I guess I'm here to figure out if you aspire to be a detective or a burglar."

Her skin burned. She could not hide the sudden flush exposing her embarrassment, but thought it was worth a try. "What on earth do you mean?"

"Come on, Elizabeth. You know why I'm here. You should also know that I could arrest you for trespassing. I know you did not break in because we left the back door unlocked on purpose, but you certainly had no business entering the property. Why don't you tell me what you were doing and show me what you took?"

Feeling small and foolish, she summoned all her dignity, and pointed to the printed papers on the corner of her desk.

"If you must know, I had an idea that there could be something on her computer that might point to a new identity, or where she would go."

"That's not bad. What made you think she would change her identity?"

"Because she'd done it before when she moved here. If she went to the trouble to make everyone think she was murdered, she couldn't go somewhere new using the same name. Once Social Security recorded her death, she could not use her identification cards again without raising a red flag. Employers can verify socials now for new employees, if she needed to work, but especially if she wanted to open a bank account."

"Good thinking," he said in what sounded like a patronizing tone, but she continued defiantly.

"So I thought if her computer was still there, I could check her history and emails."

"And what did you find?"

"Not a lot, but I forwarded her emails to me so I could look through them here. That's how I found these," she said.

He stepped over to the desk and picked them up. Reading her notes and looking at the emails, he said, "I understand about the names, but what about these emails. They look like spam to me."

"That's just the thing. One is spam, but it refers to her new Mercury MKZ. The other is a company she registered with to receive notices of raw land for sale. Don't you see? She bought a new car, and she might have purchased land that she could have built on or bought a cabin. It should be easy for the police to track all new MKZs, shouldn't it? And land sales? Then there are the emails about Venezuela. Isn't that the only country that does not honor extradition for murder?" She was so hungry right now that her stomach had a hollow, burning sensation.

"What exactly did you intend to do with this information? Start playing detective on your own to try to find her?"

"No," she said bluntly. "I had every intention of telling you what I had found. I just did not think you would take me seriously without proof, and the more I thought about it, the more I believed that she set Walt up from the very beginning. She probably knew who he was all along, and that made it even better because the revenge motive would be so strong. I wouldn't be surprised if she did not write those threatening letters herself."

"If you had called me, I would've told you that we already came to that same conclusion. I'll share something with you since you've figured out so much. We found out that Abigail Slocum had no past before she married Cyril Bradley. That leads us to believe that is not her real name. The mother she claimed to have does not seem to exist either. Right now, we don't know who Patti really is. She's the invisible woman. It'll probably take a while to gather information from police departments around the country, but we'll find her."

"But what about the woman we visited? Abigail's mother? They look just alike, except for her mother is older and heavier."

Macy let out a laugh. "What did you think of her?"

"Edgar and I visited her when Patti went missing. Then Esme, my friend, went with us when we went to extend our condolences. There's no doubt she's crazy. She didn't believe us or the cops that came to her house, but now I see that she knew Patti was alive and that we were the ones who were wrong."

"No one from the police notified her. We didn't know about her at the time. Tell me, did Walt go with you either time?"

"Walt and I went when we first learned her address, but she wasn't home. The next time, Edgar and I went. We went to ask her if she had seen Patti. She said, no. The last time, Edgar and Esme went with me. She was really off the charts nuts that day."

"The woman you spoke to in that house wasn't Patti's mother. We're pretty sure it was Patti herself."

Elizabeth looked startled. "That can't be!"

"Do you see anything significant in what you just told me?"

"No, what?"

"Suppose she didn't open the door when Walt was with you because he would've have recognized her on the spot?"

"You mean…"

"I mean, she couldn't take the chance Walt would recognize her as Patti and give the game away."

"I can't believe we were fooled," Elizabeth said. "That fat old lunatic? The place sure smelled like someone elderly and senile lived there."

"The best way to hide is under clutter. Like drug stash houses, so full of rotting garbage, dog crap, and anything else gross they can add to the mess. It's so disgusting, no one in their right mind would break in. Now, you take a little old lady, living in the clutter, the dirty diapers, and the rotting food. Who would stay long enough to scrutinize her? Anyone coming in would focus on the surroundings, rather than look close enough to notice she wore a disguise."

"Now that you mention it," Elizabeth said, "mom and daughter had a spooky resemblance. Do I ever feel like a fool. I thought she was genuine. Patti must have been laughing her ass off at us." Elizabeth tried to stop the visual, but Patti's face kept spooling in her head. "Now that you know about all the funny business, what do you do next?

"We'll send her photo out across the country to local and state law enforcement agencies, at the border, airports. She's bound to turn up. We know she hung around to impersonate her mother. That's the mystery. She had pulled off the masquerade, probably as the means to get rid of her stalker. So why hang around? But she did. If we're lucky, she's still in Phoenix. From the information you've uncovered, however illegally, we can look for the new Mercury MKZ. That tells me she's driving to wherever she's going."

"So, it was a good thing I did it," Elizabeth said proudly.

"It was, but you shouldn't be so reckless. Did it ever occur to you that Patti might still be in the neighborhood and could have seen you? After all, she'd expect the house to be unoccupied until her contents are removed. She might want to retrieve some of her personal items. She could have surprised you, and since she has nothing to lose now, one more killing probably wouldn't weigh heavy on her mind. We think we might have a chance to catch her if she returns. That's how we saw you, by the way. We've been monitoring the inside of the house with cameras to keep an eye on the property."

Elizabeth felt deflated. Between the wine and no food, her feelings of satisfaction were diminishing by the second.

"That didn't occur to me. I guess that was a bit reckless of me."

"Just a bit?"

"So you're not going to arrest me?"

"No, but consider this a warning. Real life is not like television. Sometimes an amateur gets hurt or worse butting into the bad guy's business."

"Thank you," she said, and reached out to shake his hand. She did not do humility well, but if she were wrong, best to admit it and move on. Just at that moment, Edgar knocked and walked in.

"Hello, what's going on here?"

"Oh, Detective Macy was just leaving. I'll tell you about later," turning pleading eyes in Macy's direction.

"Thank you for the information, Elizabeth. If you have any more ideas, please call me directly" He started to leave, but turned and said, "Did you come across the name Sandi DiCarlo?"

"No," Elizabeth said.

He nodded at her, and then at Edgar, and left.

"What was that all about?" Edgar gave her a severe look before he took a seat on the chair next to her. "I take it you have a tale to tell?"

"Let's wait for Esme."

"I called to offer her a ride over here, but I woke her up.

She said she ate too much and overdid the shopping today. She said she'll wait up to see you at home."

Elizabeth's face dropped. He had hoped she would be happy to be alone with him. A wave of irritation flashed over him. Antonio knocked on the office door and entered the office with their food and a bottle of wine. They scooted in around a small table against the wall, pulled up chairs, and started eating.

Edgar looked up to find Elizabeth observing him. He flushed. He wondered what went on inside her head. Estimating emotional risk, perhaps? He wondered if she could read his thoughts like she used to do—never a comfortable feeling. She averted her eyes, took another sip of wine, and adjusted her seat a few inches out of his reach.

"Detective Macy came here because he knows I went to Patti's house a couple of hours ago to search for clues to her new identity."

"You can't be serious," Edgar said.

"I *am*. I sneaked in through the back door and searched her office and computer. I had no idea they had the place staked out expecting Patti will come back. That's how they caught me in the act. No one tried to stop me while I was there. Macy just came by to let me know I'm not as smart as I think I am."

"Do you realize how dangerous that was? What if one of the neighbors had seen you. What if the cops thought you were Patti and shot you? Why didn't you tell me what you were thinking? I would've talked you out of it."

"That's why I didn't tell either you or Esme. Besides, I found something the police didn't think was important. Detective Macy took what I found, so maybe it will help them find her."

"I can't believe how casually you're talking about this. Oh, wait a minute, you're drunk."

"I admit I'm slightly drunk now, but I wasn't when I went there. Anyway, it's over. We've done all we can for Walt, and even for the police. Either they'll find Patti using an assumed name somewhere in the states, or she'll have gone to

Venezuela. Walt will move back to Corinth, Kentucky, where he really belongs. And everyone will live happily ever after."

"You *are* drunk," he smiled. "I guess I should be grateful I'm not bailing you out of jail right now."

She must have heard his irritation with the situation. "Don't act like it's your job to take care of me," she said. She waived her forefinger in front of his face, and said, "Just remember, you are not my boss."

"Calm down. I don't want to be your boss. You're too much of a wildcard. I'd have to quit my day job to keep you out of trouble."

Oh, jeez. She looks like she's going to cry. Why can't women handle alcohol?

"Listen, I'm showing my concern," he said. "That's all. Maybe too strongly. Let's calm down and eat. Enjoy each other's company."

"Speaking of enjoying my company, when are you going home to your wife?"

Edgar recoiled from the sharpness of her comment. Her eyes did not move from his. For the first time since he arrived, he realized the precarious position in which he placed himself. Here he was, trying to rekindle their relationship, all the while discounting any pain he may have caused her in the past. Now was not the time to talk about that. Tomorrow. "I planned to stay for two weeks, but I will leave sooner if I have no reason to stay."

When she did not answer, he said, "I'm going to take you home. We can talk tomorrow. Just try to stay out of trouble."

When Elizabeth walked through the front door, Esme had a bowl of popcorn and a glass of wine beside her in front of the television.

"You look terrible. What happened?"

Elizabeth dropped down on the sofa and rolled her head back. "Edgar pissed me off. What right does he have bossing me around?"

"Why did he try?"

"Because I went to search Patti's house tonight."

"What! Do we need to send out a search party to find what's left of your common sense?"

"Funny. I would've gotten away with it, if the cops didn't have the place staked out. They think Patti might show."

"Seriously? They expect her back?"

"Yes, and you'll never guess what else," Elizabeth said. She drew closer, and said, "Macy said the woman we met as Verna Kilgore was Patti disguised."

"I knew the woman seemed off, but I didn't expect that. She looked old."

"When I got into her computer, I found research she'd done to learn how to change her identity. I think she's already become someone new. Why stick around?"

"Do you think she framed Walt on purpose?"

"That would make sense if she knew who he was."

"I'm glad that's over. I have to get back home tomorrow. I hate leaving you, though. You still have a stalker out there."

"I'll be fine. I'll have a security company out to inspect my place. Put up a camera over the garage, secure the back of the house better. I'll be fine. But I'll miss you."

"You should consider moving back to Denver. You could stay with me until you got settled."

"That's sounding like a better idea all the time, but I'll give Phoenix a full year before I run back with my tail between my legs."

"Watch this movie with me. I'm glad Edgar's not around. It's nice to have girl time."

"Yes," Elizabeth said. "I need a break from him, anyway."

"Still skeptical of this yarn he weaved?"

"His mid-life crisis, you mean?"

Esme laughed. "Whatever you want to call it."

"I hear what he's saying, but after what happened before, I'm wondering how I could ever trust him. Look at what he's doing to his wife now. It's like he's scoping out the replacement before he lets the current one go. I think I'd trust him more if he had shown up already divorced. Switching off relationships so casually doesn't inspire confidence."

"I agree. So you think you'll take him back anyway?"

"I'd have to be a fool to do that, don't you think?"

"If there's anything I know about what's happened this week, it's that I'm the only one in this B-movie who isn't a fool."

"Nice talk from my friend."

"Only your true friend would be that honest. It's the truth. Taking everyone at face value, ignoring the obvious, diving in without considering the consequences. Even believing that schmuck Walt."

Saturday Morning

Elizabeth dropped Esme at the airport at seven to catch her nine o'clock flight. Her bloodshot eyes burned from crying. She hated goodbyes. She wiped her fingers over her cheeks, sniffed a few more times, and turned on the radio. The blaring music distracted her. She embraced the isolation inside the car. For the time it took to get from one point to the next, the entire world existed inside this vacuum. Anything outside did not matter.

She had a lot to consider. Patti's drama had provided enough distraction the past week and left her with little time for reflection. That might have been for the better. The situation with Edgar confused her. And her weakness to fall into the wrong relationships frightened her. She thought about what she had said to him last night. Truth in wine—as accurate a comparison as she had ever heard. All it took was for him to push the wrong button for her to give it to him right between the eyes.

She pulled into her garage, grateful again that the HOA had

found painters that were available the same day to get rid of the graffiti. After she went back to bed for another hour of sleep, she planned to start calling around for security companies. That had to be a priority. The truth was that incident had frightened her, too. Not once, but twice, getting slammed in the head. She thought it a miracle or a blessing that she did not die the second time. Maybe she would have if Edgar had not been in the front making sure she got in all right. That was a point in his favor, she thought.

The garage door finished its descent with a gentle thump of the rubber seal. Elizabeth opened the car door, grabbed her purse, but paused at the kitchen door. A chill passed across her shoulders, a strange sensation that put her neck hairs on end. The previous incident in the garage came back to her. The same sense that something was not right. The timed overhead light illuminated the room ahead of her. She looked around her but saw nothing out of place. She saw her dad's vintage monkey wrench sitting on top of her toolbox and picked it up. Just in case she was not imagining things.

She opened the kitchen door slowly, and peered through the glass for an intruder as she stepped across the threshold. Once inside, she breathed out her relief. She felt safe, but prodded herself that she should keep checking. She guessed that was her deeper consciousness alerting her, because she began to get scared again. Except this time, she had a consuming dread of imminent physical danger.

The heavy and tarnished wrench irritated her hand, but she could not let go. Her body tingled with fright. She knew someone other than her was in her house. She stood in the middle of the living room, her knees shaking, her stomach fluttering. One more step, she thought. She turned to look at the corner behind her front door. Nothing. Good. She turned around toward the hallway to the bedrooms.

Her heart came up in her throat.

Patti stood in front of her.

Elizabeth could not stop trembling. She had never been face to face with real danger before. She panicked. She could not move. Now, she could see the obvious similarities to Verna's face and build. She even detected the same madness she had seen in the older woman.

"Patti. What are you doing here?"

"I'm taking care of one last chore before I leave town."

"You're the one who hit me on the head? Why? What did I ever do to you?"

"Nothing. I wanted to punish Walt. He talked about you all the time and I'd had enough."

"That's crazy!" Elizabeth realized too late that was the wrong word to use.

Patti backhanded her so hard, she torqued her neck to the side. She went off balance, and fell backward onto the entryway mat. Patti stood over her now, kicking her in the ribs with her pointy-toed boots. Elizabeth tried to react, but the fall had disoriented her.

All she could do was take the blows that felt like they were breaking her insides. Elizabeth thought how surprising Patti's strength for a petite woman. Then the assaults stopped. Elizabeth thought she meant to leave. Instead, she reached down and raised her upright by her hair. Elizabeth screamed at the hair tearing her scalp.

Patti swung her fist with an inhuman force into her face. Elizabeth could not see for several seconds. Black and red pulses shot before her eyes. This woman intended to kill her. She had to do something. Then, she felt the scratchy surface of the wrench still in her hand. She had forgotten about it. She used all her might to swing the wrench toward Patti until she made contact with the back of her head.

Patti reeled backward. Elizabeth stood there, not sure how long she could remain on her feet. She blinked to focus. Patti came into her view, swaying back and forth before dropping to the floor. Elizabeth thought she killed her, but had no interest in finding out.

Elizabeth ran to her purse to get her phone, the wrench still gripped tightly, unwilling to let go of it. She pulled out her phone and called 911. After giving all her information, she took her phone and the wrench with her to the car, opened the garage door, and turned on the car long enough to drive it to the curb. She locked the doors, and prayed the cops got there soon.

Saturday Late Morning

This time, no one gave her the option of whether she went to the hospital. She woke up in a room, her head bandaged, something tight around her ribs, and a gross looking needle sticking out of her hand. She followed the line to a bag hanging on a metal stand.

At least I lived.

"You're awake."

Elizabeth turned her head, noticing the pain that movement caused, and saw Edgar standing next to her bed. "Hi."

"Is that all you have to say after you gave me the fright of my life," Edgar said.

"Give me a minute to think of something clever."

"Don't make yourself laugh. That might hurt."

She started to smile and realized he had a point. "Did they catch the crazy bitch?"

"Who?"

"Patti. She's the one who attacked me. She admitted she was the one the first two times. She said she wanted to hurt me to hurt Walt."

"When the police found you in your car, they checked the house. Your place is a wreck, lots of blood, furniture overturned, but no sign of anyone else."

"I hit her with the monkey wrench. She dropped to the floor. I thought I killed her or at least knocked her out."

"You better tell Macy when you see him. He stopped by earlier to check on you after he heard, but I didn't get the impression he thought this was related."

Elizabeth closed her eyes and groaned. She could not stop the flow of tears pooling around her eyes. "What if she comes back?"

"I'll get Macy over here. He needs the details."

"I guess that answers the question of why she stuck around. She had one more job to do." Elizabeth tried to put it all together. "What I don't understand is if Patti's the one who attacked me, how did she recover quick enough to come after me right after she was released from the hospital. Walt took her home, remember?"

"Macy might know the facts, but I could create the scenario like this. We know the hysteria when she came out of the safe room was an act. She planned this out. She probably figured she'd be rushed to the hospital to be checked out. They find out she was fine, just upset, so they'd give her a sedative or tranquilizer. Sure, she's off-balance. She's already talked Walt into coming with her. He takes her home."

"Okay," Elizabeth said. "What happens next?"

"He takes her home and gets her settled in. Maybe she asks for a drink or something to eat. He couldn't have been with her every second. Someone who did this extensive planning would have anticipated the drugs at the hospital. Maybe she had something on hand to counteract the sedation."

"Then, she'd have to drug Walt, right?" Elizabeth said.

"Walt had no reason to be suspicious. She could've dropped something in his drink that made him sleep. He'd think he just dozed off. He had to be exhausted, anyway. With him sound asleep, he wouldn't have known she left and returned."

"Wow. Run that by Macy when he comes back."

"I'll mention it, but I'm not too keen on telling that man how to do his job."

"Here's the thing," Elizabeth said. She rested her hand on his arm and felt a current of excitement. "I'm so happy to have seen you again after all these years. It wasn't until you turned up again that I realized how much I've missed you. I couldn't admit to myself how much you meant to me before."

"But," Edgar said. "It sounds like a 'but' is coming."

"To be honest, what you did really hurt me. I'm afraid of feeling that pain again. I can't just let the past go. You've only been back less than a week. We've talked about many things, but you know what they say about talk. It's easy, and it's cheap. You say you're dissatisfied with your life, but I'm concerned that what you're experiencing is a temporary uncertainty that will pass, and you'll regret bringing me back into your life. Aside from that, you're married. That's huge."

"You heard me tell my lawyer to get the paperwork ready to file."

"I know, but you still have your life somewhere else. Once you're home again, you might see things differently. We have a long way to go before we can be together."

"You can move back there. I'll take care of you. You won't have to worry about anything."

"Are you out of your mind? Me, become an unemployed, kept woman. That's not a strong basis for marriage, no matter how glamorized it is in some circles. I don't want to feel that I'm prostituting myself through life, and how could you respect me later if I allowed that? No, we stay on an even playing field. I have a good job here and a nice place. I'm not leaving everything behind to be somebody's whore."

"Wow, there's truth in painkillers, too. Okay, I have to understand how you feel. You're right. Can we at least agree to try this? I'll show you that I mean what I say. I'm not trying to have my cake and eat it too. I'm just afraid that now that I've found you again, I might lose you."

"You're not going to lose me as long as you keep your word."

'Pinky swear?"

Elizabeth had forgotten how they used to say that all the time. She winced to keep back the sentimental tears. "Pinky swear." She reached over and wrapped her pinky finger around his, and started to giggle. "Damn," she said, "I forgot not to laugh."

Sunday Night

Edgar leaned across the booth, moved her hair back, and kissed Elizabeth on her neck. She had warned him she did not have many spots that did not ache from the beating she took from Patti. With the pain everywhere else, the softness of his lips on her cool skin gave her ideas she kept struggling to ignore.

"Since I'm here another week, I'd like you to help me find a furnished condo nearby. I plan on coming around often, and can't stay in hotels all the time."

"Good choice. Close, but not presumptuous."

"Let's get out of here and go see a movie or something," Edgar said.

"Okay. First, I want to check on things in the kitchen. The dinner crowd should be coming in soon."

She had to steady herself before descending the stairs. She recognized the powerful effect of emotions and alcohol, with a dash of hydrocodone. At least the cool air blowing from the ducts in the ceiling had a sobering effect when it struck her face. She had almost forgotten the cap she wore to cover her head bandage, and the heavy makeup that concealed some of her facial bruising. She still had trouble believing the events of the last week. She still worried that Patti might change her mind and come back, but even that idea seemed preposterous. By now, she was on a beach somewhere getting used to her new name, and looking for her next Walt.

Downstairs, the staff were milling around at their stations, preparing for another busy night. She moved through the kitchen and behind the bar, observing them. She liked them all without exception, something unusual and unexpected in this business. She assured herself the machine was operating smoothly, and started to head back upstairs to rejoin Edgar. As she rounded the corner from the kitchen, she saw Walt sitting at the bar. Had he been there before, she wondered.

"Walt, how nice to see you. I almost didn't see you there. It must feel good to be a free man again."

"Yes, it is. I wanted to come by to tell you I'm leaving for Corinth tomorrow. And I wanted to thank you and Edgar for going out on a limb to help me. I appreciate it. If you ever need anything at all, call me."

She had to hold back from saying that she enjoyed it. "So you're going back home, then?"

"Yes. In fact, I have an early flight, but I couldn't leave without saying goodbye."

"You'll be back though, won't you?"

"I hired movers to pack up my house and vehicles, so I might not be back. Definitely not at all if my house sells quickly."

"I'm sorry Phoenix didn't work out for you, but you'll be happier around your family. You're lucky that way. So many people here don't have large families, or their families are so fragmented they don't care if they see each other or not. That's life in the big city, I guess. But you have a close family. It had to be hard to be away from them while you went through this mess."

"It's been difficult. I don't ever want to have another experience like that as long as I live, but if I do, I want to have my family around me for support." He looked as if he regretted having to leave. "Listen, I have to go now. You know how it is making sure you have everything before the last minute."

"Edgar is just upstairs in my office. I know he'll want to say goodbye."

"That's okay." Walt had an edge of something in his voice she could not identify. "Tell him thanks, and good luck. You too."

Elizabeth was surprised when, expecting a hug goodbye, instead he hopped off his stool and left quickly. She stood there, looking after him. The abruptness of his departure hurt her feelings, but did that matter in the end? He was not the right man for her; that she knew. It was time to close that door and walk away.

As if on cue, she heard the office door open upstairs and felt she had to laugh. Possibly, this was the right open door. Time would tell. Turning on her brightest smile, she hurried up the stairs with the energy and enthusiasm of a teenage girl experiencing her first crush.

Thursday Morning

As Sandy DiCarlo drove down Interstate 75 south to Florida, she checked herself in the rearview mirror and smiled. Patti Slocum and Abigail Bradley were distant memories. The woman she now saw had light auburn hair with fresh swirling curls all around her face and darkly tanned skin. With the money she had squirreled away in her safe, and the transfer of the settlement money to a numbered account, she would be sitting pretty. New wardrobe, new beachfront home, fully furnished, life was good and only bound to get better.

She hummed watching the luscious green landscape she passed along the highway. How much more beautiful this was compared to the desert. Having just stopped for another double shot cappuccino with extra whipped cream, she reached over for it and pulled off the lid so she could spoon-feed the frothy topping sprinkled with cinnamon.

She took her eyes off the road to make sure she did not spill her coffee, just as a ladder came loose from the roof of a pickup truck two vehicles ahead of her. The car in front of her braked hard, but still ran over the ladder. She slammed into the rear of that car. The impact collapsed her front end. The two cars following her could not stop either. They slammed into her in two powerful explosions, crushing her vehicle's back end like compressing a tin can. While the other passengers in the other vehicles came out without a scratch, she was the only casualty.

Thursday Late Morning

Detective Macy sat at his desk reading the results of the all-points bulletin he had on Sandi DiCarlo. Even though they solved the murders, Abigail Bradley, alias Patti Slocum, and most likely, alias Sandi DiCarlo, had eluded them. When he saw the message, he had anticipated her capture. In his mind, he had already started to plan the trip to pick her up from wherever she had ended up. When he read of the fatal accident that had taken her life, he felt shortchanged.

While this served that same end as a guilty verdict and death penalty, her death cheated the victims out of their opportunity to confront the monster and to watch her move through the grueling grind of the justice system. Not this time. They would all have to be satisfied that the nightmare had finally ended.

He looked up the number and dialed Elizabeth Kearn.

"Hello," Elizabeth said.

"Detective Macy, here. I have good news and I have bad news."

Thanks for reading my book. If you enjoyed it, please take a moment to leave me a review at your favorite online-retailer?

Connect with me on Social Sites

Twitter: https://twitter.com/feywritinggirl
Facebook: https://www.facebook.com/cathyannrogers
LinkedIn: www.linkedin.com/in/cathyannrogers
Website: http://www.cathyannrogers.com

Discover other titles by Cathy Ann Rogers

Here Lies Buried
Heavy Mascara A Short Story Collection
Cat Pistol Hoodlum, A Short Story

About The Author

CATHY ANN ROGERS has a penchant for creating literary characters who imitate reality through their skewed sense of justice as well as their bittersweet victories.

Cathy attributes the shaping of her writer's prowess to her solitary upbringing as an only child. Armed with a library card from her neighborhood branch in Cincinnati, she spent her childhood absorbed in suspenseful scenes depicted within the fiction of Christie and Conan-Doyle. Simultaneously, she built a mental library of potential plots while eavesdropping on the conversations of adults who discussed everything from Hollywood to History. The result of these blended influences is her fascination with plot twists and multi-generational storytelling in novels.

Following the dictates of her left-brain, Cathy pursued a degree and graduate certificate in accounting, establishing a tax and bookkeeping service for entrepreneurs.

Cathy weaves her tales from her Arizona desert townhome in the company of her Bichon Frises, Whitney and Sophie. She is currently working on the next installment of the Pilar Sagasta series *Here Lies Hidden.*

CATHY ANN ROGERS

DELIBERATE FOOLS

www.ingramcontent.com/pod-product-compliance
Lightning Source LLC
Chambersburg PA
CBHW021053130626
46552CB00005B/2078